Constable Over the Stile

By the same author

The Constable Series

Constable on the Hill
Constable on the Prowl
Constable Around the Village
Constable Across the Moors
Constable in the Dale
Constable by the Sea
Constable Along the Lane
Constable Through the Meadow
Constable in Disguise
Constable Among the Heather
Constable by the Stream
Constable Around the Green
Constable Beneath the Trees
Constable in Control
Constable in the Shrubbery
Constable Versus Greengrass
Constable About the Parish
Constable at the Gate
Constable at the Dam

CONSTABLE AT THE DOUBLE
Comprising
Constable Around the Village
Constable Across the Moors

HEARTBEAT OMNIBUS
Comprising
Constable on the Hill
Constable on the Prowl
Constable in the Dale

HEARTBEAT OMNIBUS VOLUME II
Comprising
Constable Along the Lane
Constable Through the Meadow

NICHOLAS RHEA

Constable Over the Stile

ROBERT HALE · LONDON

First published in Great Britain 1998
Paperback edition 2003

ISBN 0 7090 7390 9

Robert Hale Limited
Clerkenwell House
Clerkenwell Green
London EC1R 0HT

A catalogue record for this book is available from the British Library

2 4 6 8 10 9 7 5 3 1

Printed in Malta by Gutenberg Press Limited

1

There was a crooked man and he walked a crooked mile,
He found a crooked sixpence against a crooked stile.
Nursery Rhymes ed. J.O. Halliwell, (1842)

There must be dozens of different types of stile in this country. They range from simple step-ladder constructions which enable us to navigate walls and fences to the more elaborate kind which involve turnstiles, finely balanced rails or swing gates. In general, their purpose is to permit mankind to traverse the countryside by crossing walls and fences while denying the same access to farm animals. A simple V-shaped stile of stone or wood pillars will allow a person to pass through but will frustrate something as large as a cow, a horse or even a hiker with a rucksack; other stiles are designed to make things difficult for smaller creatures such as sheep and dogs and one such example is the zig-zag stile with its free swinging gate. Persuading a dog to bend in the middle so that it can pass through this stile is never easy; in fact, encouraging a dog to climb over any kind of stile is not a simple matter, hence the old definition which says that a kind person is someone who will always help a lame dog over a stile.

Persuading his flea-ridden lurcher, Alfred, to cross a particularly difficult stile on a footpath near Aidensfield was one such problem faced by Claude Jeremiah Greengrass on a mild and sunny August day.

That action had surprising results which eventually led to my official involvement as the constable of Aidensfield.

There is little doubt that Alfred was very good at leaping over fences and gates, or pushing through hedges and barriers of various types, thorny or otherwise, but a flight of rather too-small stone slabs, rising like miniature steps while protruding from each side of a high stone wall, did baffle the dog. He refused to even attempt the climb. As Claude had some pressing business at the far side of the wall, it meant he had either to abandon Alfred in the hope he would wait for his return or go home, or he would have to somehow lift Alfred onto the top of the wall from where he could leap down. At the side which confronted man and dog, the wall was too high for the dog to jump onto the top and, in any case, the approach was a steep grass slope with the wall stretching along the top. I reckoned that even a pole vaulter would have had trouble leaping over that particular wall – which explained the purpose of the curious stile.

I was to learn that Claude attempted to hoist Alfred onto his shoulder as he climbed the stile, the idea being to deposit the dog on the top as Claude completed his ascent. But the dog did not understand the technicalities of such a complex procedure and when Claude was mid-way up the stile, Alfred leapt away from him, his final kick for freedom catching Claude smartly on his head. Consequently, as Alfred leapt into the downward sloping field, Claude tumbled from the wall and reached out in the hope he could grab something which would prevent his unplanned, undignified and rather swift return to ground level.

He grabbed at one of the coping stones, but it came away from the wall. As Claude tumbled and rolled into the field, therefore, the stone fell heavily to the ground behind him. Fortunately, it missed Claude but it did crack open a ground drain which apparently ran alongside the base of the wall. Somewhat shaken, Claude picked himself up, winded, bruised but not injured, cursed Alfred in the colourful language of a poacher and then noticed that the heavy fallen coping stone was deeply embedded in the drain. Appreciating the need for rural drains to be kept clear of obstructions and showing he did have some sense of responsibility, Claude went to remove the stone with the intention of replacing it on the wall and then to cover the hole with one of the other large chunks of surplus stone which were plentiful in the vicinity. But, as he lifted the offending stone, he found it had crashed not into a drain but a pot of silver coins.

What Claude had thought to be a field drain was, in fact, a large earthenware container which had been buried with its top only a few inches below ground level. It was almost directly beneath the wall and it was full of silver coins. Not really believing his luck, Claude scooped out a handful and found they were half-crowns. This was not ancient Roman or medieval money, but current coin of the realm. And there were, seemingly, hundreds of them. . . .

The value of a half-crown was two shillings and sixpence (2s. 6d.), a crown being five shillings (5s. 0d.). There were eight half-crowns to £1 sterling and, at that time, £1 was around a day's wage for a working man. Half-a-crown an hour (12.5p in modern money) was the going rate for some rural workers.

Claude had no idea how many coins this cache contained, but a quick estimate achieved by counting ten and estimating the remainder by a rough comparison, suggested there might be several hundred . . . he knew that 800 half-crowns would be £100! A small fortune for Claude – almost three months' income in fact.

Whatever the urgency of his mission at the other side of the wall, it was forgotten in those moments of absolute euphoria. For a few minutes, Claude was content to squat on the ground and scoop handfuls of coins from the hole in the ground; he allowed them to trickle through his fingers while Alfred sniffed at them to determine what was so intriguing to his lord and master. Then, having satisfied himself that no human being had witnessed his discovery, Claude used his hands to scoop up the entire cache and spread the money about his person in the many capacious poacher's pockets of his old overcoat. The cash fell into his pockets with what Claude regarded as heavenly music; it was the sound of immense riches all in cash. When he had emptied the earthenware container, he decided he would take that too. With great care, he eased it from the ground and found it was in five broken parts, all fairly large pieces. When complete, the pot would stand about ten inches high and be about the same width at the widest part; the neck was narrow and so was the base. It was the sort of kitchen utensil some farmers' wives would use to store pickled onions or preserved eggs. In spite of the damage, Claude felt the pot could be repaired. Being a man who bought and sold what he described as antiques, he reckoned the pot might bring a few shillings, even if it was damaged.

Having extracted every piece of pottery from the large hole in the ground, Claude refilled the cavity with small loose stones, kicked some loose earth over the top and finished the job with a large stone covering the lot. By the time he had finished, no one could have guessed that this slight disturbance in the ground had recently contained anything, most certainly not a cache of silver coins.

Having satisfied himself that he had collected every single coin – all half-crowns dating from 1836, in the reign of William IV – Claude whistled for Alfred, abandoned his original mission and, rather furtively, hurried home with heavily laden pockets and his pieces of pottery.

One can only speculate upon his actions when he returned home with his treasure. I imagined him sitting at his table like Scrooge, running his fingers through a pile of silver coins while he wondered what on earth to do with them. Finding a hoard of this kind is one thing – dealing with it effectively is another. Claude, however, was bright enough to realize that if he began to pay his bills and buy his drinks with nothing else but William IV half-crowns, then someone would begin to ask questions about the source of his money. And if people began to discuss Claude's sudden wealth and his apparently endless supply of half-crowns, then folk memories of the hidden cache might be revived – and someone might come forward to claim the money. After all, it was quite clear the money had not been lost – quite clearly, it had been deliberately concealed in that hiding place. The snag was that Claude had no idea when it had been concealed, but the fact it had been positioned so close to the foot of the stile meant the site could easily be retraced and the money recovered.

Certainly, the coins were of a considerable age – they were more than a century old and all minted in the same year, that fact being rather strange – but they could have been buried very recently. I am sure Claude's mind began to work along the lines that if his discovery was made public, either locally or on a wider basis, then someone would come forward to claim the cash, either by saying it had been stolen from them or that they had hidden the cash for reasons best known to themselves. The appearance of a possible owner was something Claude did not want – he believed in the old adage of 'finders keepers'.

I do know that he kept his secret for several days, neither spending any of the money nor talking about it to anyone. He placed all the coins in a hessian sack and concealed them under a floorboard in his sitting-room; the broken pot was left in one of his outbuildings with no attempt to repair it. For a while, therefore, the money was something of a problem and even a worry for Claude, and I have no doubt he scanned the local papers and listened to gossip for news that someone had tried to recover the cash, only to be welcomed by a hole full of stones and earth. But there was no outcry, no publicity, nothing.

By one of those flukes of circumstance, it was around that time there was a spate of road building. Motorways and new major roads were being constructed throughout the country, large housing developments were appearing, too. One outcome of all this was a lot of earth-moving activity which in turn led to the regular discovery of ancient ruins – Roman settlements, stone-age camps, the foundations of medieval buildings – and buried treasure.

Bronze-age bracelets, a gold torque, an 800-year-old statuette, silver spoons, silver plate, a hoard of old pennies, Roman coins, gold coins and silver coins – in fact, thousands of pounds' worth of treasure was being unearthed on a surprisingly regular basis and this received widespread publicity in the newspapers. In many cases, the finders – often farmers and farm workers – found themselves with a fortune. And Claude Jeremiah Greengrass read most of these accounts.

He read one story about a gold coin worth £1,700 being found in a field; he read about a hoard of thirty-five silver coins worth £7,000 being unearthed on a building site, and sweated over a report about a farm worker whose plough turned up £50,000 worth of silver coins. And in all cases, these discoveries had been subject to the law of treasure trove. Claude quickly understood that if something comprising gold or silver was found in circumstances which suggested it had been deliberately hidden, then the law of treasure trove had to be obeyed. The find must be reported to the police who would notify the coroner, then an inquest would be held to determine whether or not the hoard had been deliberately concealed. If it had, then it must be handed to the state, through the British Museum, and the finder would be paid the full market value of the discovery. In most cases, that would exceed the face value of the found coins.

If the treasure had not been deliberately concealed, for example a solitary coin found beside a public footpath, or a gold ring found buried in a garden, then such items had probably been lost and not deliberately hidden.

In such cases, they might belong to the finder, or perhaps to the owner of the land in question or to the loser if he or she could be traced. But, Claude learned from these reports, if the finder of treasure did not report it to the authorities, then the entire hoard could be confiscated and the finder would get nothing, except an appearance in court for concealing the discovery of treasure trove. Honesty, he learned, was by far the best policy in the case of gold or silver treasure. In any case, the finder could earn more from the British Museum that he could by concealing his discovery. Armed with this information, therefore, Claude approached me. I was patrolling the quiet main street of Aidensfield when he emerged from the pub with Alfred in tow. I stopped when he hailed me.

'Ah, Constable,' he beamed, his eyes blinking rapidly as he confronted me. 'Just the man I want to see.'

'That's a change!' I retorted. 'It's usually me who wants to see you. . . .'

'Aye, well, this is different, you see,' and his old eyes flickered and darted about as he decided how much he should or would tell me.

'I'm listening,' I said, waiting.

'Well, I've been reading a lot about treasure trove, you know. In the papers, that is. Folks have been finding fortunes in fields and on building sites.'

'They have indeed.' I had read most of the items. 'Lucky for some!'

'So if somebody finds silver coins, they should report it to you?' he put to me.

'That's right,' I said. 'And I will report it to the coroner who will hold an inquest. . . .'

'I thought they were for dead folks?' he frowned.

'An inquest is an enquiry.' I explained the history and reason for inquests to him, ending with, 'So it's far, far better for someone who has found a hoard of silver or gold to report it. There's a fortune waiting in most cases – while those who conceal their discoveries risk losing the lot and getting nothing.'

'Aye, well, that's what I thought, Constable.' He paused, his eyes blinking away as he looked first at the ground and then up in the air and then from side to side. 'Well, you see, I've found some coins. In an old pot. Over by Carr End Wood.'

'Ah, I see!' I waited for him to reveal the rest of the yarn. He then told me of his experience on the stile and how he had come to find the pot of coins.

'So they're all half-crowns?' I asked.

'Aye, but old ones. 1836. That's the date on 'em. That's going back a bit, Constable.'

'How many are there?' was my next question.

'Six hundred and forty,' he beamed, his eyelids moving up and down like miniature shutters. 'That's eighty pounds, Constable. Face value, that is. Face value, not what they might really be worth.'

'Whose reign is that?' I asked.

'It says Gulielmus IIII D.G. on the front,' he said. 'Sounds like somebody foreign to me.'

'That's William IV,' I told him. 'It's Latin. D.G. means *Deo Gratias*.'

'So they're English?' he said. 'I thought they were mebbe Welsh or Scottish or summat, with that funny name.'

'Right,' I said. 'I'd better collect them sometime, or you could bring them to me. I'll give you a receipt and will set the procedures in motion to fix an inquest, then you can find out just how much they really are worth.'

'You can come for 'em now if you want.' He was suddenly very enthusiastic about the whole idea and so I decided to accompany him to his ranch. On the way, however, we had to pass Cowslip Cottage, the home of a retired gentleman called Alec Hughes. Alec was our local coin expert. On several previous occasions, I had sought his advice about coins found buried around the village, particularly when it came to identifying very old ones or attempting to establish their source.

'Claude,' I said as he reached Alec's gate. 'I want to ask Alec about your coins. Come with me, and tell him about them.'

Almost bursting with pleasure and anticipation, he followed me to the door. Alec responded to our knock and invited us into his cosy dining-room; the table was covered with a thick velvet cloth across which were spread a selection of dirty silver coins.

'Philip and Mary shillings,' he said. 'I'm trying to get one sample of each one. But what can I do for you, Mr Rhea and Mr Greengrass?'

'Claude has found some half-crowns,' I introduced the matter. 'He'll tell you about them.'

Once more, Claude gave a highly embroidered account of his discovery, concluding with a description of the half-crowns.

'Most unusual, Mr Greengrass,' said Alec. 'Most unusual, to find so many all of one date . . . now, let me see. . . .' He pulled a catalogue of British coins from a shelf and turned to the reign of William IV. Half way down the page was a black and white photograph of a half-crown, showing the obverse and reverse.

'That's the one!' Claude was almost jumping up and down with excitement as he prodded the picture with his finger.

'1836, you said?' added Alec.

'Yes. All of them have that date on them.'

'I find this most intriguing,' said Alec. 'Not necessarily the date but the fact there are so many all bearing the same date. Now, Mr Greengrass, if your coins are in perfect condition, they could be worth anything between fifteen and twenty pounds each.'

'Each?' he almost shrilled.

'Yes, a William IV half-crown in EF condition – that means Extra Fine – is worth around that amount. Say fifteen pounds per coin to be the lower side. Now, if the coins show wear, even slight wear, then the value drops dramatically, in this case to some eight or ten pounds per coin, and for those with considerable wear and use, the value drops to something like two or three pounds per coin. But you know the laws of treasure trove? You must hand them in, Mr Greengrass, but you will not be out of pocket, by no means. So yes, you have a valuable hoard on your hands. I congratulate you.'

'You've no idea how they might have come to be hidden like that, have you?' I asked.

'Sorry, Constable, no idea at all. I confess I am totally baffled by the fact they all bear the same date. That is most unusual . . . most unusual indeed. I wonder if someone has collected them because of the date? Perhaps the date was of some significance to that person? If not, then I am most intrigued. There is only one other explanation for them all having the same date. So, is it possible I might have a look at them?'

'Aye, the constable's coming with me now, to collect them, and then he'll set the official wheels in motion.'

'I'll bring them straight here,' I promised Mr Hughes.

'And I'll come an' all,' beamed Claude.

In Claude's cluttered and dusty living-room, I waited as he prised up the floorboards to reveal the bulky hessian sack. Lifting it out, he passed it to me as he relaid the boards and I took it, then peeped inside. It was extremely heavy and I could see the mass of coins. I shook the bag to make them settle, but I did not think the sound they produced was like modern coins. It was a dull noise, not the nicer sound of silver coins being shaken about. But I said nothing. Perhaps older coins did not have the lovely clear ring of their modern counterparts?

Twenty minutes later, we were back at Alec's cottage. I allowed Claude to carry in his precious load and, in the meantime, Alec had cleared the table of his own collection. He invited Claude to pour his treasure onto the tablecloth so that each coin could be examined. Again, I noted the dull sounds produced by the coins – and so did Alec Hughes.

He looked at me quizzically and I opened my hands in a gesture which he interpreted as one of understanding. I knew what he was thinking. Alec picked up one of the coins and bit it.

'Hey, you can't eat 'em!' smiled Claude. 'I know they're tasty morsels and they're going to make me rich, but you can't eat 'em, Alec.'

'Mr Greengrass,' said the gentle man, 'I am afraid I have some bad news for you. . . .'

'They're only worth a fiver apiece, is that it? 'Cos they're worn round the edges?'

'No, they're not worth anything. They are valueless, Mr Greengrass, because they are not genuine coins. They are counterfeits, made from base metal . . . see, it's softer than real silver, there's a lot of lead in it . . . I wondered whether that was the case when you said they all bore the same date. That's one clue to counterfeit coins – a counterfeiter makes a mould, you see, from a single coin, and everything that emerges from that mould is identical . . . so you've a bag full of duds. I'm afraid. I'm so sorry, Mr Greengrass, so very sorry for you.'

'Duds?' he almost cried. 'But why would anybody hide duds?'

'Because their activities had been discovered perhaps? They wanted to hide the evidence . . . coining was a serious crime, Mr Greengrass, with the death penalty in some cases, years ago. . . . Now, I have no idea when or where these were made, but they are counterfeits. I'm sorry.'

'Well, does that mean they're worth nowt?'

'Absolutely nothing, Claude,' I said. 'In fact, they're a liability. There's a whole range of offences covering the possession of counterfeit coins so you have to surrender them. They will be destroyed.'

'I was going to surrender them anyway. . . .'

'Better luck next time?' I said, helping Alec to replace the coins in Claude's sack.

'What about the thing I found 'em in?'

'That might be worth a bob or two,' I said. 'And it's not subject to the law of treasure trove.'

'Aye, but it's broken!' he grumbled, the disappointment clear on his face. 'It'll not sell for a lot, and getting them things repaired is never a simple matter.'

'You could always bury it again,' I smiled.

'And fill it with stones, you mean?' He suddenly grinned. 'Just in case whoever made them coins comes back for 'em?'

'A nice idea,' I said, taking the coins from Alec Hughes. 'Sorry, Claude.'

'Mebbe I should have hung onto them and tried to spend 'em. . . .'

'I think not,' I said. 'For once, Claude, your obedience of the law has saved you from further trouble. I'll give you an official receipt and will let you know when they been formally destroyed.'

'Thanks for nothing! And you can keep the sack,' he muttered, as I carried the heavy load outside.

If Claude's expectations had risen momentarily due to the finding of his evaporated treasure, then the same could never have been said about young Christopher Kitson's fruitless search for silver. Chris, as everyone called him, was fifteen; the son of Andrew and Anita Kitson, he was an only child and had developed into a rather serious, music-loving youth who did not enjoy being with a crowd. He was well known around Aidensfield because, during the week, he delivered newspapers from the village shop before travelling into Strensford to attend the grammar school. At weekends, he often visited his grandfather, did his shopping or took the old man out for a trip in his wheelchair.

Chris preferred to play his violin rather than football or cricket and, while the other lads of his age would be rushing off to local matches or village dances at the weekend, Chris was happy to sit with a book, walk alone on the moors or practise his classical music. Tall, good-looking and with a delightful sense of humour, he was a likeable lad who did not get teased like other youths who had sensitive temperaments. There is no doubt that through his charm and humour, he could deal effectively with anyone who might be tempted to bully or tease him – and he had no shortage of girlfriends. He was a lad who knew his own mind and was not afraid to follow his own instinct rather than be persuaded by pressure from his peers.

As the village constable, I was well acquainted with Chris. Often, I'd see him during the early mornings going about his paper round and he'd always smile and bid me good morning. In many ways, he was the ears and eyes of Aidensfield, visiting more houses than I during the course of his working week.

One of his strengths was his ability to respond to minor events along his delivery route – on several occasions, he told me about milk standing on doorsteps for longer than usual or elderly people not opening their curtains. Once he told me about someone who had gone away on holiday and left the cat locked in a bedroom and another time, how holidaymakers had departed leaving the oven on. On his daily rounds, Chris had noticed these things and had wisely alerted me or the relevant families. In this small way, and in many other ways, he showed initiative coupled with a welcome sense of responsibility.

Like most of us in Aidensfield, we knew of the close relationship between Chris and his grandfather, old Kit Kitson. Old Mr Kitson, also baptized Christopher but known to all as Kit, lived alone in a cottage on the green, his wife having died several years before my arrival as the constable. Kit managed to look after himself surprisingly well in spite of having to use a wheelchair for his outings – a back injury sustained during his work as a woodsman had caused his disability. In the house, though, he could struggle about his daily routine without the chair, although Anita, his daughter-in-law, did help with his washing and cooking. It was when Anita had undertaken this work in the early days of the loss of Kit's wife, that young Chris had gone with her and the friendly relationship between grandad and grandson had developed.

At weekends especially, Chris would spend hours with his grandad who, in spite of working in the tough role of woodsman for a local estate, also had an artistic streak.

He liked ballroom dancing and dance music, loving the big bands of his era and possessing hundreds of records of his heroes like Victor Sylvester, Eric Delany, Glenn Miller, Ted Heath and other masters of dance music. In his fitter days, Kit Kitson would travel miles to dance – which is where he had met his late partner, Iris. From dancing the modern waltz, foxtrot and quickstep in local village halls, Kit had established himself as such a good dancer that he'd been sought as a partner for ladies who wished to dance competitively, in both the old time and modern styles. And so dancing had been his life – always supported fully by Iris. He had also once played the trumpet in a local dance band, the Moortones. The Moortones played regularly in villages across the moors, their 'home' being Milthorpe Village Hall with its wonderful sprung floor. This hall, set in remote moorland, was favoured by hunt balls, wedding dances, annual dinner/dances and similar important events – invariably with music by the Moortones.

Due to Kit's wide knowledge of ballroom dancing in all its modes, he'd been asked to judge many competitions across the north-east of England and had acted as MC at important events in some of the area's finest hotels and dance halls. As MC, Kit had had to wear an evening suit with highly polished black shoes, and it had been his job to organize and call the dances, establishing his authority with a silver whistle.

But his back injury had put an end to all that. Now, well into his seventies and unable to dance any more, he enjoyed his memories and his recorded music.

There is no doubt he was so pleased he could share these with his grandson. Fortunately, young Chris did enjoy music of all kinds and although he had not shown any desire to acquire his grandfather's skill in ballroom dancing – to my knowledge he had never been to any of the local dances – it was due to his grandfather's influence that he decided to learn an instrument. This had led to his ability with the violin.

Then someone decided to stage an old time dance at Milthorpe Village Hall.

Although the new rock-'n'-roll dancing and its vigorous variant was popular, the older people preferred the classic style of what had become known as old time, or even 'olde tyme' dancing but opportunities had become fewer for dancing the valeta, the dashing-white-sergeant or the lancers or even a modern waltz and foxtrot. The majesty and polished skills of that beautiful age had vanished in the noise of pop-singers' discs accompanied by wild and unco-ordinated acrobatics.

The Milthorpe Old Time Dance was the idea of Molly Potter. She hailed me in Aidensfield village street one Monday morning and told me of her proposals, adding that it might be a good idea to have intoxicants for sale during the dance. She sought my advice on the legal aspects of that idea, and I explained accordingly. The suggested date for the dance was Saturday, 20 September and I said I would note it in my diary so that either I, or other police officers from Ashfordly, could patrol the village to ensure there was no trouble.

'That's our only worry,' she said. 'I do know that troublemakers are likely to turn up and cause fights, but there's no way I can stop them coming, is there?'

'You could make it ticket-only admission,' I said. 'And make them so expensive that none of the rabble would want to bother to come. Or you could form a club – the Milthorpe Old Time Dance Club – and then limit the event to members only who bought tickets in advance. That way you could pick and choose your members and keep the rabble away. It would make life easier for you and for the police.'

'That's an idea!' she said. 'A dance club . . . yes, Mr Rhea, I like that.'

In that casual way, the idea for a dance club was formed and Kit Kitson found himself being invited to become president. He accepted with great delight and on the Friday before the big dance, I happened to see young Chris delivering his morning papers in Aidensfield.

'It's your grandad's big night, eh?' I smiled. 'His first event as president of the new dance club!'

'He's really looking forward to it,' grinned Chris. 'And he's taking me. He wants me to see what real dancing is like, so he says. Dad and Mum are going as well; we're all going in their car. Grandad has been asked to MC the lancers, just like he used to . . . he's found his whistle and is busy swotting up all the moves!'

The dance was a huge success with 120 people attending and not one iota of trouble. Such was the happiness it generated, that it was scheduled to become an annual event, and word of the new dance club in Milthorpe soon spread with people from neighbouring villages applying to join. There would be regular club nights too. But during the following days, I noticed a change in young Chris Kitson.

The first intimation was sight of him walking across the moors from Milthorpe, using a well-established path which crossed the fields and moors; via this route, Milthorpe was only a couple of miles from Aidensfield, whereas the route by road was nearly four miles. It would be about ten days after the dance and I was visiting a farm on the edge of the moor above Milthorpe. I spotted his lonely figure trudging along the path with his head down and his hands in his pockets. It was half term, so I knew he was not playing truant.

'Isn't that young Kitson?' I commented to the farmer, Frank Mitchell.

'Aye, it is; he's been up there a few times this week,' replied Frank. 'Allus alone, head down like that. . . .'

'He's like a poet creating a poem!' I said. 'Or a composer working on a tune.'

'It's a pity he's got nowt better to do,' grinned the farmer. 'I could use a spare hand if he's looking for summat to occupy him!'

'He's usually busy with something or other.' I tried to protect the lad because I liked him. 'It's not like him to mooch about like that.'

'Well, at least he's not doing any harm to anybody,' said Frank. 'Not like some that use that path, setting fire to t'moor or leaving rubbish behind.'

During that week, I realized that Chris Kitson was spending a lot of time walking alone and in apparent misery along the path between Aidensfield and Milthorpe and although I accepted his behaviour was none of my business, I did have some concern for the lad. If something was bothering him, he should not have to deal with it alone. An opportunity for a chat with him came the following Friday.

It was almost a fortnight after the dance and I was undertaking an early foot patrol of Aidensfield. I came upon Chris who was walking briskly towards the railway station with his satchel of newspapers. I knew he delivered one paper at the station and another at Beckside Cottage half a mile or so beyond, and so I fell into step beside him.

'Hi, Chris,' I said. 'Mind if I join you?'

'No, not at all, Mr Rhea.'

'I'm on an early route,' I explained. 'Our office makes us do these early patrols once in a while, to make sure we get out of bed! We have a set route to walk, usually over a period of four hours. I started at six this morning.'

'I like the early morning,' Chris smiled. 'Everything's so fresh. I don't have to get up so early during half term, but I enjoy the mornings and don't like lying in bed all day.'

'I saw you on the moors the other day,' I said. 'I was visiting Frank Mitchell at Rock Head Farm; you were walking along with your head down as if you had the worries of the entire world pressing on your shoulders!'

He turned and smiled at me; it was a wan smile, then he lowered his eyes and blinked and I could see something had upset him. I halted. Quickly, I looked around and established that we were alone on the edge of the village. Knowing that our conversation could not be overheard, I asked, 'Is something wrong, Chris? Something bothering you?'

The slight movement of his head indicated that something was troubling him and, after taking a deep breath, he turned to me and said, 'Mr Rhea, you can keep secrets, can't you?'

'Yes, I can. We're trained to respect confidences.'

I waited and then he began to walk again, heading in the original direction and I strode to keep pace with him. I decided not to press him to reveal the cause of his distress – if he wanted to share his burden with me, then he would do so – and I did not lose sight of the fact that he was only fifteen years old.

'You know my grandad, Kit Kitson?' were his next words.

'I do indeed,' I smiled. 'A wonderful man, Chris.'

'Yes, he is and I adore him, Mr Rhea. I would hate to do anything that would upset him. . . .'

'I can imagine how you feel,' I said.

'You know about his dancing, and when he was MC?'

'I knew he had done that sort of thing when he was fitter,' I acknowledged.

'Well, he had a silver whistle, Mr Rhea. Real silver, it was. He used it during his MC work, blowing it to control the dancers; he's had it years. It was specially made, Mr Rhea, a dance MC's whistle, with his initials on it. He was really proud of it.'

'He never showed it to me,' I admitted.

'Well, you know the Milthorpe Dance? A week last Saturday?'

'I do indeed, a very happy event.'

'Grandad did his MC bit there, Mr Rhea, calling for the lancers, but with his injured back and his age, he said he didn't think he could ever do it again. It was a long time since he'd done that sort of thing and he found it very tiring. He told me he would retire there and then. And he did.'

'A nice way to end his dancing career.' I struggled to find a suitable comment.

'Well, the day after, Mr Rhea, the Sunday it was, I went to have my usual chat with him and he gave me that whistle. That really surprised me. He wanted me to have it. He knew I'd never be a dancer like him or an MC or anything, but he wanted me to have it. I was really proud, Mr Rhea.'

'And?' I knew there was more to come.

He took a deep breath and halted in his walk. 'I've lost it, Mr Rhea. I can't find it anywhere . . . and I daren't tell anybody, not my mum or my dad – and certainly not my grandad. . . . I mean, he kept it all those years and I've lost it so soon . . . it was very precious to him, Mr Rhea. I don't know what to do. I've looked everywhere. I've got to find it.'

'Is that what you were doing when I saw you?'

He nodded. 'Yes, after he gave it to me, I put it in my trouser pocket and I went for a walk to Milthorpe that Sunday evening . . . I'd met a girl, you see, at the dance, and said we'd meet up. . . .'

'And was she there? The girl?'

'Yes, we walked over the moor and talked. She was nice. I'm going to see her again, next Sunday.'

'What's her name, Chris?' I wanted to know this in case there was any question of the whistle being stolen.

'She's called Carol. Carol Fletcher. She likes music, Mr Rhea, like I do. She plays the piano. We get on well.'

'And the whistle? Did you tell Carol about it? And about your grandad?'

'Yes, she was interested. I told her all about his dancing days and what he used the whistle for. I showed it to her.'

'And you're sure you returned it to your pocket?'

'Yes, Mr Rhea, I was extra careful. I put it in my left pocket, with my handkerchief and loose change. I have a little wallet in the other pocket; I keep birthday money in it, notes that is, and reminders about birthdays and things.'

'So what about that Sunday night when you went home? Was the whistle there then?'

'I never checked, Mr Rhea. When I went up to bed, I didn't turn my pockets out, you see; I never do that. I got undressed and got into bed, then next morning got up, delivered the papers and went to school. I never checked for the whistle then – to be honest, I forgot about the whistle when I was delivering and when I went to school.'

'Could anyone steal it at school?' I put to him.

'Not that Monday, no. We didn't have gym or sports, they're on Wednesdays, so I didn't have to leave my clothes unattended in the changing rooms.'

'And you never saw it again? So when exactly did you notice it was missing?'

'This Monday after tea, when I went up to my room. We're off school as it's half term. I suddenly realized I hadn't seen the whistle. I can only think I must have pulled it out of my pocket with my handkerchief or something. I've searched my room and grandad's house where I sat and the loo and the places I walked with Carol in Milthorpe and that path across the moors. I've been back time and time again, Mr Rhea, to all the places I've been since he gave it to me, but haven't found it. I've checked at school as well, in my class-room and where I've played and had my music lessons, and all along the village street at houses I call at with papers.'

'And you haven't told anyone about the loss?'

'No, how could I? If my grandad finds out, he'll be so upset. . . .'

'We do have a lost and found property department, Chris. If someone loses something, it's often worthwhile contacting the police, then if the object is handed in, we can match it with the loser. We do restore a surprising amount of lost property to the rightful owners.'

'Oh, I had no idea but, well, I can't let my parents know, can I?'

'Right. Give me a description of this whistle and I'll check our found property registers. At least it's a start and you could be lucky. Somebody could have found it and handed it in, especially if it's obviously something unusual or rather precious.'

Chris described the whistle as being about an inch and a half long and rather wide or squat in shape – three-quarters of an inch or so.

There was a half-moon shaped hole in the top and the mouth was shaped to accommodate a person's lips. At the back end there was a small split ring which would take a chain or string and the entire object was made of real silver. It had a slightly uneven surface bearing a carved foliage-type of design and there was a hall-mark at the back, near the split ring, but he did not know its lettering or design. On a small shield-shaped area on the top were the initials C.K. in copperplate engraving, meaning Christopher Kitson.

'You won't tell my folks or grandad, will you?' he pleaded with me.

'No, of course not,' I assured him. 'Right, I have to visit Ashfordly Police Station this afternoon so I'll check our found property registers. If the whistle has been handed in I'll make sure it comes back to you without anyone knowing.'

Sadly, there was no record of Chris Kitson's whistle, but I did make an entry in the Lost Property Register in the hope that someone might find it and report it to us. Feeling sorry for the lad, I did a brief tour of the half-dozen or so antique and second-hand shops in Ashfordly, asking about the whistle and describing it to the shopkeepers, just in case someone had found it and sold it, but again drew a blank. It began to appear that young Chris would have to be honest with his grandfather and admit to losing the heirloom.

I returned to Aidensfield that Friday afternoon, but did not make the mistake of visiting the Kitson household to relay the bad news to Chris; instead, I would await the opportunity of catching him in the street and I managed to do this on the Saturday morning.

He was delivering the papers and noticed my approach in the Mini-van, waiting to speak with me. I eased the van to a halt and climbed out.

'Sorry, Chris,' I began. 'There's nothing in our records, and I called at the second-hand shops too – but no luck.'

'I have to see Grandad tomorrow,' he said gloomily. 'He left a message with Dad; he wants me to take the whistle back as he's got a pal coming for tea and wants to show it to him.'

'Oh dear,' I sighed. 'So it's hands-up and be-honest time, is it?'

'Yes,' he said. 'I feel so awful, Mr Rhea. . . .'

'You've been over all the ground again, have you? Revisiting all the places you've been to since he gave it to you?'

'Everywhere, Mr Rhea. School, home, the street – and Carol and I must have searched every inch of the path between here and Milthorpe.'

'It could still be in your house.' I was speaking almost to myself, and then I had a brainwave. 'You said you might have pulled it out with your handkerchief?' I reminded him of an earlier suggestion.

'Yes, I did that once. I sneezed, whipped my handkerchief out and the whistle came with it, and fell onto the floor. I heard it fall that time.'

'So if you could pull it out like that, so could someone else,' I said.

'Nobody uses my handkerchief, Mr Rhea!' he said with some disdain.

'But I bet your mum digs into your pocket when she wants to do the washing,'

I suggested, 'When's washing day?'

'Mondays,' he said quietly. 'Yes, she goes through my pockets for handkerchiefs on Sunday nights, and I leave my other stuff on the bed on Monday mornings.'

'Has she a washing machine?' was my next question, thinking that if the whistle had fallen into the works, it would have jammed or, at the least, caused some kind of obstruction.

'Yes, one of those new twin tubs,' Chris said. 'But she puts all the dirty washing into a big basket first and sorts it. . . .'

'I think you need to search that basket, the drying ground of your garden and anywhere else your handkerchief might have got to, even the washing machine and its pipes,' I suggested. 'Even if the whistle was wrapped in your hanky, it might have fallen out during some stage of the washing process without your mum noticing it.'

'I never thought of that,' he said, with some show of relief and gratitude. 'Thanks, Mr Rhea. I'll do it the moment I get back.'

To cut short a long story, Chris rifled the dirty washing basket and found his whistle. It had become wrapped in his handkerchief as his mother had removed it from his pocket and she'd not noticed. The handkerchief had been placed in her dirty washing basket and then, as his mum had lifted out each item to examine it and grade it as whites or coloureds, the whistle had slipped out to fall without a sound onto the remaining clothes, from where it had worked its way to the bottom of the heap of clothing.

There it had remained undiscovered for almost a couple of weeks – it would have been found eventually, I am sure, but only if Mrs Kitson had completely emptied the basket. And that happened on very rare occasions.

Understandably, Chris was mightily relieved. He told me he would save his paper money to buy a silver chain so he could hang the whistle on it from a hook on his bedroom wall. There it would remain in full view until it was required and then he'd wear it around his neck.

As I said to young Chris Kitson the next time I saw him, 'Your efforts to recover the family heirloom were well worth the whistle.'

'Is that a quote from Shakespeare?' he asked with a smile.

'To answer that one, you'll have to launch another search,' I laughed.

2

The joys of parents are secret, and so are their griefs and fears.

Francis Bacon (1561–1626)

It was a long time before I realized that Mr and Mrs Bentham of Thornfield House, Aidensfield, had a son. So far as I was aware, the well-off, affable and very likeable couple, now in late middle age, had no children – none lived with them, in my recollection none had ever called to see them and there was no evidence of any grandchildren. No paddling pools were stored in the outbuildings, no toboggans lingered in the garage and no beach balls awaited discovery in the garden borders. Young people never seemed to be invited to the house and none of the village children was ever invited there to play or have parties.

However, the Benthams did not dislike children or young people; on the contrary, they appeared to enjoy contact with them at events such as the school's Open Day or fêtes in the village. Nonetheless, they lived the kind of life which did not involve young family members or grandchildren and which, in addition, implied they were comfortably off with no financial worries. Certainly, their home, Thornfield House, was a gem; set on a hillside in seven spectacular acres overlooking the dale below Aidensfield, it was built of local stone with a pantile roof and boasted six bedrooms, two bathrooms, a double garage, conservatory and three reception rooms in addition to a south-facing kitchen.

Being the local constable, I wanted to know about the couple and discovered that Leonard Bentham had retired early due to ill-health.

A stout man of average height with broad shoulders, a good head of fair hair and a distinctive moustache, he was noted for the smartness of his expensive attire and the magnificent old silver-coloured Alvis car he used constantly. He had been only fifty-two upon retirement, but, at the time I was the village constable at Aidensfield, he was in his early sixties. In spite of his health problem, he looked quite fit, but he had a serious heart condition which could be aggravated by stress or undue physical activity. To prolong Leonard's life, his doctor had recommended he desert the turmoil of London in favour of the calmness of a home on the North York Moors with lots of fresh air and the opportunity for gentle, physical exercise. And Leonard Bentham had heeded that advice, coming with his wife to live in the village a few years prior to my arrival.

He and his wife, Alice, had quickly settled into Aidensfield life and were popular residents, both serving on the parochial church council of the Anglican church and involving themselves with charities and local events such as the annual Blessing of the Plough or village fête. They provided valuable support for national charities and both served on a selection of local branch committees, ranging from the Red Cross to the Royal National Institute for the Blind via Aidensfield Flower Show and Ashfordly and District Motor Club.

Over a period of months, I learned that Leonard had worked in London as a barrister where he had specialized in income tax matters and he'd made sufficient wise investments to be able to retire early. This, like his health problem, was no secret – he had explained it many times to friends in and around the village.

I believe he had inherited money from his parents and from an uncle, too, and thus the rather premature termination of his career did not impose any financial strain upon him. Indeed, he continued with some consultancy work for which he received a handsome retainer and substantial fees and thus he was able to potter around his small estate and occupy himself in a gentle, meaningful way which did not threaten his health.

Alice, his wife, was more active in the village and beyond than her husband. Younger than him by a couple of years or so, she was a slim, well-dressed and highly attractive woman with long dark hair tied at the back in a pony-tail, who liked to wear full-length, flowing dresses, rich with pastel colours. She worked as a consultant in colour co-ordination, giving advice to large stores, hotels, stately homes and similar places of renown. In spite of her high reputation in that profession, she did not ignore the village's needs and was regularly asked for her ideas of up-to-the-minute colour schemes for the village hall, the pub and even the local shop – and she obliged, giving her expertise free of charge.

Most of my contact with the Benthams came through visits to the house in the course of my work. Leonard Bentham owned a .22 rifle and a shotgun which he used on his land for the destruction of vermin and this meant I had to make periodic visits to his home to renew the respective certificates. From time to time, there were other reasons to call at the house – to warn against confidence tricksters or unscrupulous workmen offering their doubtful services, for example, or to discuss various village matters.

These included such knotty problems as the serving of alcohol to the public at church events or the management of traffic if a visitor-friendly fête was held on the village green. The Benthams were away from home quite a lot, too, sometimes for just a single night during the week and occasionally for weekends or a longer holiday. Whenever this happened, I would be asked to keep an eye on their house and invariably there was a thank-you card in my letter-box the day after their return. Whatever the reason for my visit, I was always made to feel welcome; as the local people invariably said, 'There's no edge on the Benthams, they're really nice folks.' And so they were.

On the occasions I had visited the house or spoken to the couple, there had never been any reference to a family. It was not the normal subject for a conversation unless, of course, there was some common ground. If they'd had a son about my age, I am sure they would have discussed him with me, particularly if he had entered the law as his profession. I calculated that if they'd had children, then they would be about my own age or perhaps a little older – in their late thirties perhaps. The chances were that if they did have children of that age, there would be grandchildren around the age of my own young brood – but that topic was never raised and I never asked. It wasn't the sort of thing one discussed without invitation, although I was aware that I had never seen or heard the voices of little ones at Thornfield.

As if to reinforce their childlessness, I did notice that no family photographs adorned the mantelshelves; neither were there any on display in any of the rooms that I had visited – although I had never ventured into any of the bedrooms.

Added to this, neither of them mentioned any family – thus I assumed, quite naturally, that Leonard and Alice Bentham either had not wanted or could not have, any children. The matter was not a talking point; it was an accepted fact and no one in the village ever considered the Benthams' lack of family to be any way unusual. But quite unexpectedly, the situation changed.

A local painter and decorator mentioned in the pub that the Benthams' son was coming home after several years of working abroad. He knew that because he'd been asked to redecorate the son's bedroom at Thornfield House. This was the first anyone had heard of a son and initially, those who heard the painter's version thought he was imagining it or that he had misunderstood some other information. Then Joe Steel, from the shop, came up with the same story – Leonard and Alice Bentham's son was coming home shortly after a long time working overseas. Little else was known at that stage, but Joe was adamant that the tale was correct – he had been told by none other than Leonard Bentham himself.

It was Joe Steel who then passed the news to me.

'Are you sure?' I asked, wondering why there had never been any previous reference to a son.

'Sure as I'm standing here talking to you, Nick,' affirmed Joe. 'Leonard told me himself. He said his son is coming home after a long spell abroad; Leonard came here to say he intended to increase his regular orders for bread, vegetables and so on. "One extra mouth to feed in the very near future", he said. And he's had the lad's bedroom redecorated, to make it more suitable for a man rather than a youth.'

'Well, if he told you, it must be right,' I had to admit.

'He said it won't be permanent, Nick. His lad has ended his contract and will be looking for other work; he was with a civil construction firm apparently, building roads and bridges. If he gets work either here or overseas again, he'll be off once more, but I got the impression his folks expect to have him around the place for a few weeks until he gets himself fixed up with something.'

News of the impending arrival of the hitherto unknown son of the Benthams did generate a good deal of excitement in Aidensfield. The cricket and football teams wondered whether he was a good player or any use as an umpire or referee; available young women in the village (and their mothers) wondered if he was single, good-looking and wealthy in his own right; some of the smaller local businesses, particularly those associated with the building trade, wondered if he had skills to offer them, while Aidensfield garage felt he might like to buy a car or a motor bike if he was going to remain a while. The Women's Institute wondered if he would give them a talk about his experiences overseas; the vicar thought he might have time on his hands which would enable him to cut the grass in the churchyard and weed the path, while the parish council felt it should arrange its next election of members to cater for his arrival. And lots of others had their own plans for the young fellow when he arrived – after all, the darts team at the pub was usually short of good players and there was always room for a thrusting and confident person on the village hall committee. Thus, in its own way, the impending arrival of Bentham junior was of great interest to many Aidensfield residents.

Soon, we learned that his name was Jeremy Hugh Bentham, that he was thirty-three years old, unmarried, six feet tall with the dark hair of his mother and her rather slender build. He liked sports, so we discovered, and was keen on squash and badminton. Far-sighted young women with rose-tinted spectacles did not lose sight of the fact that one day he could inherit Thornfield House and the wealth that went with it; consequently, some of the dress shops in Ashfordly did a roaring trade in new outfits while the hairdressers, likewise, reported a brisk trade ahead of the impending arrival of Jeremy Hugh. Variations of this kind of speculation buzzed around and enlivened the village for a couple of weeks with no sign of the eagerly awaited young man, and then, quite unexpectedly, I was summoned to a meeting with Sub-Divisional Commander, Inspector Harry Breckon, at Ashfordly Police Station. I had no cause to even consider that this meeting might, in some way, be connected with the impending arrival of Jeremy Hugh Bentham.

Because there was no explanation for the meeting, which was to be on the following Wednesday at 11 a.m., I wondered what on earth I had done wrong and visualized being posted to some far-flung corner of the North Riding of Yorkshire or whether someone had made an official complaint against me. All manner of such eventualities crossed my mind as I motored into Ashfordly and parked my Mini-van in the police station yard a few minutes early, My concern had prompted me to dress in a smart uniform and even to get my hair cut – such formal meetings with one's sub-divisional commander were not everyday events.

When I entered the police station, PC Alf Ventress was working at the enquiry desk and both he and Sergeant Blaketon were just as worried and as intrigued as I; both knew about the meeting, but neither knew its purpose.

As I walked in, Blaketon said, 'Rhea, what's this all about, getting the inspector to come out here for confidential words in your ear? Have you been up to something? Rocking the boat? Upsetting members of the public, our customers? Asking for a transfer?'

'No, Sergeant.' I spread my hands to indicate my lamentable lack of knowledge. 'I have no idea what this is all about. I just hope they're not posting me to South Bank or somewhere just as bad.'

'I used to be at South Bank, Sarge,' muttered Alf. 'A dreadful place.'

'For young and ambitious constables, Rhea, South Bank is one of the best training grounds in our force area,' Blaketon countered. 'Industrial areas like that, rich with humanitarian problems, domestic activities and hard-drinking steel workers, and located on the edge of Middlesbrough's teeming metropolis, can teach you a lot. If you do get posted there, don't object. It'll be a prelude to promotion, Rhea; it'll teach you a bit about real police work. You can learn more during one Saturday night in South Bank than years on a rural beat like Aidensfield. And if you want to get yourself promoted, you need that kind of experience. You can't buck the system, Rhea, so if the powers-that-be want you to go, then go you must, without questioning them, without asking why. Obedience, Rhea, official obedience!'

'I'd rather be posted to Hull!' muttered Alf.

We discussed the likelihood of a move to pastures new, even if those pastures were covered with concrete, council houses and blocks of flats, and even if the move was deemed necessary for career purposes. During our deliberations, Inspector Breckon's Ford Consul pulled into the police station yard. Moments later, the great man emerged. He plonked his cap on his head and came to our office front door. Within seconds, he was striding into the office where Blaketon, Alf Ventress and myself stood rigidly to attention.

'Morning Sergeant, morning Ventress, morning Rhea,' he smiled as he entered. 'All correct?'

'All correct, sir,' returned Blaketon. 'Nothing untoward during the night. No crimes reported.'

'Excellent, Sergeant, that sort of thing always keeps the bosses happy at headquarters. Now, PC Rhea, let's go into the sergeant's office. And you, Sergeant Blaketon, had better join us. And, PC Ventress, I think a sample of your station coffee would not go amiss. Three cups if you please.'

'Three cups of best Ashfordly nick coffee coming up, sir,' grinned Alf.

The inspector was a happy, confident fellow in his late forties. With some twenty years police service in uniform, he was a very capable man whose knowledge and common sense I appreciated; should I ever need career advice, or even some help of a very personal nature, then I would never hestitate to seek a word with Inspector Breckon. I knew I could rely on his advice. But this time he wanted to see me – and I had no idea why.

Placing his cap on the side of Blaketon's desk and a blue folder beside it, he settled in the chair and for a few minutes, as we awaited Alf Ventress's renowned coffee, he and Blaketon chatted about professional matters, particularly as they related to Ashfordly section. There was talk of amalgamations with other police forces, talk of boundary changes at both national and local level, talk of closing sectional stations like Ashfordly in favour of a merger with Eltering with a group of police stations being under the sole command of a chief inspector.

Such talk was, at that time, fairly common-place, but I did know that there was an element of truth in it. The Boundary Commission had made certain recommendations which included, among other things, the establishment of a new county called Cleveland which would embrace industrial Teesside and include large areas of the North Riding and County Durham. In our region, there was to be another new county called Humberside which would span the River Humber and encompass parts of Lincolnshire, the West Riding of Yorkshire and most of the East Riding. Worse still, the abolition of the three Ridings of Yorkshire had been suggested. Yorkshire without the North Riding, West Riding and East Riding was unthinkable ... but the proposals were based on that kind of radical, unrepresentative and illogical thinking and, if they were implemented, the police forces of the area would have to endure dramatic changes with the smaller forces being absorbed within the larger ones. The future looked bleak – it promised a good deal of turmoil along with some jockeying for positions of authority by ambitious police officers which, they hoped, would lead to promotion.

Such was the talk prior to the arrival of Ventress's coffee and I began to wonder if I was to be involved with those changes. Perhaps a posting to headquarters to become involved with the administrative work surrounding that dramatic upheaval?

When the coffee arrived, it halted all such discussion; I don't think it was anything to do with the quality, taste or curious appearance of the liquid in the cups, rather it was due to the fact it was time to proceed with the business of this meeting. As we stirred our coffee, enhanced by ample amounts of sugar, Alf took his leave, raised his eyebrows at me in a gesture which registered his curiosity, and closed the door behind him. I wondered if he might linger awhile outside in a brave attempt to determine the reason for all this secrecy.

'Well, let's get down to business,' said Inspector Breckon, picking up the blue file and opening it before him. As the file fell open, I saw the words 'Highly Confidential' across the front. 'You'll be wondering what all this is about?'

'Yes, sir, I must admit we are,' said Blaketon.

'Well, it is of more concern to PC Rhea, but I felt you ought to be made aware of the contents, Sergeant,' began the Inspector. 'Now, PC Rhea. You have a family living on your patch, in Aidensfield itself, by the name of Bentham?'

'Yes, sir,' I agreed, and, anxious to display my local knowledge, added, 'Leonard and Alice Bentham; they live at Thornfield House. He's a retired barrister, sir, he retired due to ill health and she is a colour consultant, very respected in her profession. They used to live in London and came to live in the area because of the calm lifestyle of the moors.'

'I suspect he came for other reasons if the truth was known,' said Breckon. 'Well, PC Rhea, you have not mentioned his son? Jeremy Hugh?'

'He's due home any time now, sir, he's been working overseas for a number of years. He's coming home to look for fresh work, possibly in this country. He is thirty-three, unmarried and quite good at sport, so local intelligence informs me.'

'Your local knowledge is impressive,' smiled the inspector. 'But, sadly, you have been rather misinformed. Jeremy is coming home, PC Rhea, but not from overseas. He's coming out of prison. An English prison. On licence. He's been inside for the past twelve years, doing time for murder. He's a lifer.'

'Murder?' I could not prevent myself calling out the word.

'He's a convicted murderer, Rhea. Now, I must tell you that there was a strong case for convicting him of manslaughter rather than murder. According to this file, the jury discounted the defence submissions that the evidence supported a verdict of manslaughter and he was convicted of murder. Afterwards, some newspaper reports said the jury was prejudiced against Jeremy because he was from the professional classes and had had a public-school education, but the upshot was he got the mandatory sentence for murder – life imprisonment. You know how unreliable and biased some juries can be, especially when they think something has been influenced by class distinctions, but the judge realized what had happened. His response was to recommend leniency due to the exceptional circumstances, and that is why Jeremy has been released on licence after serving only twelve years.'

'What did he do, sir? Am I allowed to know?' I was shocked by this revelation and on the spur of the moment could only think of that question.

'There was a fight outside a night club in London. Some yobbos attacked Jeremy and his pals – Jeremy happened to be carrying a flick knife which he used to defend himself. The thugs used boots and fists, and so when Jeremy's knife severed an artery of one of them, he found himself arrested for murder because the chap died. The argument was that Jeremy did not meet force with like force – the prosecution, quite rightly, argued that a fist is no match for a knife. The fact he was carrying the knife – something not disputed in court – influenced the jury and they believed he had gone out with the deliberate intention of stirring up trouble and using it. Jeremy said he always carried it: he was a keen angler and used it for gutting fish and so forth. The judge, in his summing up, did try to steer the jury towards a manslaughter verdict based on the self-defence issue, or even a justifiable homicide verdict, but the jury would have none of it.'

'So Jeremy's education and upper-class accent got him a life sentence?' I said. 'That shows the supposed fairness behind left-wing socialist attitudes!'

'That's one interpretation. The other is that the old pals' act has provided him with a rather early release – his father was a barrister, remember, and was well acquainted with most of the judiciary. Whether or not his early release will prompt friends of his victim to seek him out for further revenge is something I do not know, but the purpose of this meeting, PC Rhea, is quite simply to let you know that a convicted murderer is coming to live on your patch.'

'Have I any official role to play?' I asked.

'It is a condition of his licence that he reports any change of address or personal circumstances, like getting a job or marriage, to the police – to you, in this case. He has already nominated his parents' address as the place he will live upon release. There might be other conditions to his licence, like reporting to the police once a month, or liaising with the probation service. Those details have not been finalized – or if they have, I have not been informed.'

'I'll keep an eye on him, sir,' I said.

'I don't think that is what we have to do, PC Rhea. The reason for this meeting is merely to acquaint you with the fact that you have a convicted murderer, released on licence, living on your patch. I must add that this information is highly confidential. No one outside this office must be made aware of Jeremy's record – so you must live with his secret, PC Rhea. He is not regarded as violent or as a potential re-offender, but if he does commit any other relevant crime, then, of course, he will be in breach of his licence and could be returned to prison. He knows that, of course.'

Breckon then passed me a photograph of Jeremy Bentham and I could see the likeness to his mother. Although this was an official prison photograph, the man did look like a professional person rather than a professional villain. It would not be difficult to recognize him when we met. I could now understand why his parents had left London for a new life in the remoteness of the North York Moors, and I could see how they had planted and nurtured the idea of a son working overseas.

To some extent, I could even understand why they had not displayed any photographs of him. I guessed that any such photos had been carefully retained in his bedroom, a sort of shrine to his memory, secure from public scrutiny. To display them in a place where visitors could see them was a means of inviting questions, which they did not want. In their own way, his parents had done, and were doing, all in their power to help their son; having given him support in the past, now they were faced with helping him to reintegrate into society. I could also understand the reason for their frequent absences from home – they would have been visiting him in prison. But they had ensured that Jeremy and his unfortunate past were not known in this part of the world. Thanks to the careful ground-work by his parents, Jeremy could reconstruct his life as he wished – he had no earlier reputation to live up to. And I had no desire to obstruct him in his attempt to rehabilitate himself.

Breckon added that the file would not be lodged at Ashfordly Police Station, and said that no one else must know of Jeremy's past. Apart from his parents, the only two people with a knowledge of his criminal record would be Sergeant Blaketon and myself. I departed from the police station in something of a daze and with Alf Ventress clearly dying to know what had transpired at the meeting, but I left him in blissful ignorance as I drove home wondering how I would cope if any of my children became involved in serious crime. I hoped I would find the strength to provide all the love and support they might need.

As I approached the village, I realized that Jeremy was about my own age . . . he'd need male company of his own peer group, so could I become friends with him? Knowing his past, would I buy him a drink in the pub, or join him in the cricket team, or would I be able to treat him as just another ordinary young fellow in the village? Would I worry if I saw him at a village dance or, more especially, if I found him arguing with thugs?

Would I become concerned if he joined any of the activities in the area? In short, I knew I had to treat the man as an equal – but I knew that would not be easy.

In pondering those questions and while contemplating my future conduct, I began to think that my police experience in Aidensfield was infinitely more educative and interesting than any Saturday-night shift in industrial South Bank, with or without the complications of hard-drinking steel workers.

Then, first thing the following morning, I received a telephone call from Leonard Bentham.

'Ah, PC Rhea. Glad I caught you. My son is coming home on Thursdav next and I think you and I need to have a chat about it. As you know, I do have a legal background which makes me believe you might already be aware of his impending arrival.'

'Yes, I am aware of it and I do know the background. I can call this morning,' I said. 'How about eleven o'clock?'

'Yes, that will be fine,' said Leonard Bentham. 'Coffee will be on.'

And thus the rehabilitation of Jeremy Hugh Bentham began in Aidensfield.

Another person with a secret was Adelaide Powers, Miss Adelaide Powers to be precise. A spinster of the parish of Aidensfield in her mid-sixties, she was a retired headmistress of a Midlands grammar school who had returned to the village of her youth to occupy the former home of her parents. They had died some years earlier, leaving the house and contents to Adelaide, and their departure from this earth had enabled her to return to the village after a busy teaching life. Adelaide, an only child, had in fact been reared in the house which, in the past, had been owned by her mother's mother. Thus the female line of this modest dynasty had lived in Glebe House for a century or more. No one knew the fate of the house once Adelaide left this world because she had no children, although one village elder felt there were some distant cousins in Scotland who might eventually surface. Adelaide, of course, could make a will and leave her house, contents and money to the local cats' home, but most felt sad that such a lovely old house should end its long association with Adelaide's family.

The house occupied a quiet site on the edge of the village. Behind it was an orchard with apple and pear trees which also contained a garden shed, summerhouse and goldfish pond, and a garden with rows of soft fruit bushes and a spacious vegetable patch. The house was large and roomy, being built of local stone with a tiled roof; there was a conservatory on the western wall in which grew a grape vine, while the double frontage sported splendid bay windows and a fine porch over the solid oak front door.

Furnished with antiques, it was a very comfortable home and Adelaide was very happy there. Having been headmistress of a busy school, she liked having people around her and there was usually someone or some event in the house – meetings of the Art Club were held in her spacious lounge, she hosted occasional meetings of various working parties of the parish council; she had ladies in for sherry, lunch or afternoon tea; she started a Local History Society with meetings in her house and had regular reunions with former colleagues, some of whom came to stay for the weekend to enjoy outings to the moors and coast.

It is fair to say that many of the village people had, at some stage, been visitors to Adelaide's house and that included both me and Mary, my wife. Mary helped with the children's playgroup; the playgroup used the village hall for its twice-weekly activities for which a small rent was required and, because Adelaide was treasurer of the village hall, Mary had to visit her from time to time to pay the required fees. My own visits were fairly regular, too, sometimes in connection with village-hall business, and sometimes due to my involvement either officially or privately with one or other of the organizations for which Adelaide held some responsibility.

I liked her. She would always produce a cup of tea or coffee and invite me to stay for a short chat. Being well-read, she had a wide knowledge and deep interest in current affairs as well as the history of both Britain and Aidensfield and I must say I did enjoy our chats. It made a welcome change from being bombarded with people's opinions about parking tickets, speeding fines and litter louts.

Adelaide had a very tall and dominating presence, which might explain her success as a teacher. I couldn't imagine any class or individual getting the better of her! A large lady with a big, round face, iron-grey hair, horn-rimmed spectacles and a liking for loose-fitting dark dresses, she possessed a strong voice which both demanded attention and commanded respect and yet she was kind, tolerant and helpful to everyone. Even the village children liked her, but they never tried to take advantage of her kindness – rather, they respected her. They would never raid her orchard for apples, for example, or play noisily on the green outside her house. Some of them would run errands for her and, in return, she would take them into the house for lemonade and buns. I had the impression that Adelaide was a most capable person, one who would not tolerate fools and one who was not afraid of anything or anyone. I could imagine her dealing very effectively with anyone who trespassed in her house and grounds or who offended or obstructed her in any way.

But she endured one deep, deep fear – and it was a long time before I appreciated her phobia.

It was Mary who first realized all was not entirely well with Adelaide. Mary went to Adelaide's house one fine Tuesday morning in July for the usual purpose of settling the village-hall dues, but there was no response to her knocking. In such cases, Adelaide had given all her callers specific instructions – 'If I don't answer the door,' she often told them – and Mary – 'I'll probably be in the garden. Come down the side of the house and shout for me. If I'm not in the garden, then you might have to come back another time.'

And so Mary did just that. She walked along the path which ran beside the house into the orchard and garden at the rear, and she called Adelaide's name. It was evident that Adelaide was somewhere on the premises because the back door was standing open; there was a wheelbarrow on the lawn, a pile of weeds on one of the footpaths and a variety of garden tools strewn about the place.

Mary called her name and eventually there was a muffled reply; Adelaide had shut herself in the garden shed. Puzzled and wondering if someone had locked her in for a joke, or whether Adelaide was ill, Mary opened the door to find Adelaide cowering on a garden chair. She was pale and shaking all over, but made a determined effort to stand up as Mary attempted to go to her aid.

'Adelaide? What's the matter?' Mary was very concerned, as she told me afterwards. 'Shall I get the doctor? The nurse? Some tablets maybe? Are you supposed to be taking something?'

'No, no, I shall be all right, Mary. Quite all right,' and Adelaide popped her head out of the door, peered around the garden as if checking that the cause of her distress had disappeared, and then took a deep breath. Whatever had terrified her had disappeared and the colour returned to her cheeks in moments. Soon she was completely normal and smiling at her visitor.

'Sorry about that, Mary. Now, come into the house; I keep the papers in there as you know.'

'Should you get a check-up, Adelaide?' Mary asked but Adelaide steadfastly refused all offers of help.

She then attended to Mary's minor item of business in a perfectly normal manner, offered her coffee and then returned to her garden chores without explaining the reason for her lapse. Mary came home rather worried about Adelaide, but I assured her she'd done all she could without being intrusive, although I did make a mental note to mention her experience confidentially to either the doctor or the district nurse if I encountered them. As things worked out, I visited Adelaide myself before I had the opportunity to mention her problem to either the doctor or the nurse. And I found her in the garden shed.

My experience was almost identical to that of Mary. Adelaide was cowering behind the closed door of her old garden shed as if she'd been faced with something too horrible and ghastly to describe and, after poking her head out of the door upon my arrival, she recovered in moments and dealt with my enquiry as if nothing had happened. Like Mary, I asked if she wanted any kind of help, from a doctor perhaps, or anyone else, but Adelaide shook her head and refused to discuss the matter. I noticed her attacks had not occurred in the house and wondered about the significance of the garden shed. Whatever had terrified her, I noted she had taken refuge in the shed – not the house or any of her other outbuildings. A brief and almost superficial examination of the shed during that visit showed it to be a perfectly normal structure, built solidly of wood many years ago, with a felt-covered wooden roof secured to two stout beams, a glass window in one side and a good solid door. It was large enough to accommodate all her tools, wheelbarrow, lawn-mower and such, as well as her garden chairs and a metal table.

At home, I discussed my experience with Mary who told me she'd heard a similar tale from another lady in the village. Mrs Angela Welford had called on Adelaide some weeks previously and had found her quivering with fear in the garden shed, but there had been no explanation from Adelaide.

I realized that this was something of a very personal nature and likewise knew that I must not interfere. Whatever was causing these dreadful panic attacks was something she alone must deal with – and so she did, by enclosing herself in the garden shed. There seemed to be no other method for her to cope with her problem. I began to wonder about the mystery of her garden shed.

Some three or four weeks later, I encountered the district nurse, Margot Horsefield. Our respective duties coincided when an old man collapsed in the village street in Aidensfield, immediately in front of a passing car. Luckily, the driver of the car managed to stop without running into the casualty so neither was injured. Margot and I, both working in the village at the time, were on the spot within minutes to deal with the incident. The collapsed man was a holidaymaker who'd suffered a heart attack. He survived thanks to the good care he received in Strensford Hospital, although the driver of the car started to blame himself for the incident. We had difficulty explaining he was in no way responsible – in fact, his quick reactions had saved the casualty from further injury and removed the need for me to submit a road traffic accident report! It was after discussing the case that I decided to mention Adelaide to Margot.

'I know about it. It's a phobia of some kind,' Margot told me. 'She refuses to talk about it – I've found her in the garden shed too, with the door shut, on more than one occasion. But whatever it is that terrifies her, it's gone in seconds. It does not follow her into the shed nor does her terror last very long. She recovers in minutes. But she always runs for shelter in the garden shed, Nick. Don't ask me why; there's nothing there except garden tools and so on. No bottles of gin or other comforters.'

There was no reason for me to be unduly concerned about Adelaide. For one thing, it was not a police matter and another factor was that her peculiar condition was known to others, including the district nurse. As a consequence, I tried to put this minor concern to the back of my mind.

Then one hot summer morning, I had to visit Adelaide in the course of my duty. She had provided a reference for a young woman who wished to join a Scottish police force and, as was the practice in all such cases, the reference had to be checked to ensure it was genuine and I was on my way to her house with a copy of the reference to verify. I knocked on the door, but there was no reply although it was evident she was about the premises. As was the practice, I walked along the side of the building and headed for her garden, but the moment I emerged from the shadows of the house, I saw a fluffy white cat stalking across the lawn. Adelaide was hoeing weeds in one of the borders and chanced to turn in my direction as I approached. Then she saw the cat.

She shrieked in a manner which told me she was utterly terrified of the animal, dropped her hoe and fled, panic stricken, towards the shed. The cat, alarmed by her sudden, noisy reaction, bolted into the vegetation as Adelaide slammed the door to enclose herself in her place of safety. Everything happened in a matter of seconds, but the picture of Adelaide's reaction to her dread remains with me to this day.

Somewhat surprised by this turn of events, I halted in the

middle of the lawn and found myself staring at the old wooden shed and at the area where the cat had vanished. The garden was as still as a morgue for a few seconds. Then I decided I should approach Adelaide. I went to the shed, tapped on the door and opened it. She was sitting on a garden stool with her head in her hands, shaking like a leaf.

'Adelaide? Are you all right?' I asked.

'Has it gone?' She did not look at me nor did she remove her hands from her eyes.

'The cat, you mean? Yes, it's gone,' I said.

She removed her hands and remained on the stool for a moment or two, taking deep breaths and trying to get herself back under control.

'I'm sorry.' She shook her head. 'I am really sorry, Nick, behaving like that, but I can't help it . . . they terrify me. I am petrified of white cats . . . I cannot even look at one . . . you must think I am stupid.'

'Most of us have phobias of some kind.' I tried to sound sympathetic and understanding. 'An aunt of mine went to pieces whenever she saw a spider and lots of people can't stand rats or mice; and there's a friend of mine who can't touch feathers on a bird, dead or alive.'

'We're a funny lot.' She appeared to have made yet another of her rapid recoveries. 'But with me it's only white cats. Black ones, tortoiseshells, marmalade cats . . . I'm fine with those. But white ones really frighten me. It's so silly, really.'

'But why run for shelter into the shed and not the house?' I asked. 'If you're in the shed which is in the garden, then that white cat could be around for a long time. If the cat decided to go to sleep in your garden, you could be marooned in your shed for hours!'

'Oh, we always ran for the shed,' she said shrugging her shoulders.

'We?' I puzzled.

'My mother and my grandmother – and I think her mother before that . . . we always ran helter-skelter for the shed when a white cat appeared.'

'All of you?' I puzzled. 'All of you afraid of white cats?'

'Well, I've often wondered why we all made such a fuss when a white cat appeared.' She looked rather sheepish now, chatting in such a way to me. 'It doesn't make sense because we never did when other cats came along, but I ran because my mother ran, and I think she ran because her mother did . . . I don't think any of us really asked why, come to think of it. I grew up thinking I had to run for safety every time a white cat appeared – I have no idea what it might have done to me, but can remember my mum and my granny grabbing my hand and screaming at the sight of one, then running into that shed.'

'And, down the generations, all of you ran into the shed! That very shed, was it?' I asked. 'Every time?'

'Yes, it's a very old shed.' She patted the woodwork. 'I think my great-grandfather made it.'

'I can't understand why you sought refuge here.' I shook my head. 'There must be a reason, Adelaide.'

'Oh, there is,' she said smiling quite blandly. 'It's the wood. This beam,' and she patted a beam above her head. It was directly over the door, running the width of the shed. 'It's rowan wood, Nick. The mountain ash, some call it. It saves you from cats.'

'But that's an ancient moorland superstition,' I told her. 'Rowans were supposed to avert witches and witchcraft or diseases and prevent the effects of the evil eye, not merely keep you safe from white cats. Farmers planted them near the house and close to their outbuildings, like the cow house and stables, their presence was supposed to avert all manner of mishaps. If you take a good look at some of the older farms on the moors, especially the outbuildings, you'll see beams of rowan wood still in place. It's for much the same reason that some houses and buildings have horseshoes fastened to the wall, or why brides carry horseshoes on their wedding day, or why we adorn the house with greenery at Christmas . . . they're all ancient superstitions lingering in our modern world.'

Years ago, the moorlands in which I lived were rich with witchcraft beliefs and one very common method of frustrating the activities of witches was to make wide use of the rowan. The stocks of whips used by horsemen were made of rowan, some wove sprigs of rowan into the manes of the horses; milk-churns were made of rowan to help butter-making, babies were laid in cradles made from rowan wood; pigs were thought to thrive if a garland of rowan leaves was placed around their necks; farm tools of various kinds had rowan-wood handles and beams of rowan were placed across doorways to protect those within the buildings . . . and here was a fully grown, intelligent woman still, albeit unwittingly, thinking that a beam of rowan would protect her from the unknown evils brought by a white cat. In England, a white cat was often thought to bring bad luck – but it brought good luck in America; over there, black cats are considered unlucky.

Now she had explained a little about her actions, Adelaide's strange behaviour made some kind of sense. In those highly superstitious times a century and more earlier, some female ancestor of hers had clearly believed that any white cat was a bringer of misfortune and, upon seeing one, had panicked and taken refuge in the nearest building which boasted a piece of rowan wood. If she'd had her little girl at her side, then the child was also whisked unceremoniously into shelter – and that shelter happened to be the garden shed. I imagined that successions of little girls had been rushed into that same shed by frantic mothers whenever a white cat appeared . . . and so, even in modern times, echoes of that ancient superstition lingered in Aidensfield.

Adelaide offered to make me a cup of coffee as I discussed the document which had resulted in my presence that morning and I accepted. But the talk over coffee was about many of the curious superstitions and practices which lingered on the moors and how many of them survived without their followers appreciating the reason for some of the procedures they followed. Quite simply, it seemed, Adelaide had been conditioned from her earliest moments to be afraid of white cats, and she had continued that fear into her adult life without ever pausing to think of a reason. Following our chat, I think she began to take stock of her behaviour.

'Next time I see a white cat in the garden, Nick, I will do my best not to run for shelter in the shed, I promise you. I will struggle to confront it . . . touch wood I won't be afraid any more . . . if only I can stand still long enough for the thing to go away before I turn and gallop into the shed. . . .'

'I wish you luck,' I responded, showing her my crossed fingers.

3

Revenge is a kind of wild justice, which the more man's nature runs to,
the more ought law to weed it out.
Francis Bacon (1561–1626)

If the opportunity for revenge ever presents itself, some of us who have been seriously aggrieved may find it very difficult to resist. Whether it takes the form of spitting into an aggressor's face, putting itching powder in his clothes, arranging for a funeral cortège to appear at his house while he is entertaining friends, chopping the tops off all his cabbage plants or doing something infinitely more terrible, the act of revenge can sometimes appear to be very satisfying. Getting one's own back, the popular name given to the act of retaliation for some past wrong, large or small, is by no means a rare event and history is full of magnificent examples, yet wise people know that revenge can prompt an escalation of pointless vengeance in return.

Most of us know the ancient advice, given in the Bible, that we should turn the other cheek if someone hits us and the poet Oliver Wendell Holmes (1809–1894) reminds us of this when he writes: 'Wisdom has taught us to be calm and meek, to take one blow and turn the other cheek.' But he adds, 'It is not written what a man shall do if the rude caitiff smite the other one too!' 'Caitiff', by the way, is an old word for a base or despicable fellow, or a coward.

One serious outbreak of revenge in which I was involved at Aidensfield served to remind me of the words of Lord Byron who wrote: 'Sweet is revenge', but, he added, '– especially to women'.

In those few words there are echoes of the oft-repeated adage 'Nor Hell a fury like a woman scorn'd'. In the Aidensfield case, it involved Michael Barton and his wife Eileen. They lived in married happiness at Ash Tree House, a pretty but very compact detached dwelling in the centre of the village not far from the garage. Of modest size, with three bedrooms, it had a pleasing garden with a greenhouse, but it was by no means a mansion. Compared with many, it was a modest house. But it was home for the Bartons and they had struggled over the years to buy it, furnish it and maintain it. They were living there upon my arrival as the village constable and, so far as I know, they had occupied the house since their wedding some twenty-two years earlier. The Bartons had two children, a son of twenty who was in the Royal Navy and a daughter of eighteen who worked as a nurse in London. They came home from time to time and I gained the impression that they were a very close family.

A rather quiet couple in their mid-forties, the parents did not involve themselves with village matters, preferring to spend their leisure time either at home or eating out in one of the lovely old inns which they found as they explored our moors. There is no doubt the demands of their business occupied most of their time, both at work and at home and I am sure this prevented their wholesale entry into Aidensfield life.

The Bartons owned a hardware business in Ashfordly. Known simply as Bartons, it had grown from a tiny, one-room shop in a side street to a large, fully stocked emporium just off the market place.

Bartons sold everything from kitchenware to lawnmowers and even stocked parts for bicycles and spares for washing machines and vacuum cleaners. There was an astonishing range of screws and a bewildering choice of springs. The success of the business was due to years of hard work from Michael and equally to years of support from Eileen. In the early years, when they were struggling to find the money to buy stock and to expand their range of goods to cater for the modern public's demands, she had worked in all kinds of other shops, earning cash to feed and clothe the children, and allowing Michael to plough his earnings back into the business. And their self-sacrifice was successful. Bartons was known throughout the district and the shop's motto had become a local catchword - it was: 'If we haven't got it, we'll get it'.

In spite of their success, Michael and Eileen Barton never boasted and, even as their business blossomed and expanded, there was no discernible difference to their lifestyle, except perhaps that Eileen's clothes looked a little more expensive and Michael took to drinking wine instead of beer. Another distinction was that the cheaper furnishings within their house were replaced with antiques of undoubted quality. In addition to the antiques they bought, Michael had an antique grandfather clock, a chest of drawers, a refectory table and a carver chair, some of which were heirlooms and some of which he bought when he'd had sufficient funds. Then came a show of wealth. One Christmas, Michael bought himself a brand new Jaguar 3.4 saloon in brilliant red, and Eileen acquired a lovely MG sports car with a solid top. That was in bright red, too, with a black roof; a pair of red devils as someone joked. They were the couple's Christmas presents to one another.

It was the February following the arrival of those two splendid, head-turning cars that the weather turned extremely nasty with heavy snowfalls, blizzards and drifting during the day, with hard frosts at night. Having listened to the forecast one Tuesday morning as heavy flakes drifted from the heavens, Michael decided to take the bus into Ashfordly. He said he'd not risk his precious new Jaguar on the moorland roads that morning. But, during the day, the weather worsened. Roads were blocked with drifts, power lines were brought down and many moorland communities, including Aidensfield, were cut off. People were marooned at their places of work and vehicles of all kinds were being abandoned on many of the more exposed highways. By tea-time that day, all the roads into our village were blocked in spite of the snowploughs working non-stop to keep them clear. Our telephone lines were down and the electricity supply had been interrupted countless times. In order to maintain my own contact with the outside world, I relied on the radio in my Mini-van – I kept it switched on in the garage as I worked at home, switching it off from time to time to conserve the battery, when I walked into the village.

Then, around 5.30, I received a call from Alf Ventress. He was radioing from Ashfordly Police Station with a request message from Michael Barton.

'I've got Michael Barton with me in the office, Nick,' he said. 'He's marooned in Ashfordly due to the weather. Can you tell his wife? He can't ring her because the lines are down. Just say he'll get digs in the Black Swan for the night and will ring as soon as the lines are reconnected. In any case, he'll be in his shop tomorrow.'

'Right, no problem,' I said.

Dressing in my waterproofs, I trudged the short distance to Ash Tree House and Eileen answered my knock. I gave her Michael's message, but was rather puzzled by her reaction. I got the impression there was a hint of suspicion rather than relief at what I was saying, even though I had opened my conversation with up-to-date comments about the atrocious conditions on the moor.

'The Black Swan, you say?' she asked, with an unaccustomed hardness on her face.

'That's what he told our man in Ashfordly,' I repeated.

'OK, thanks, Mr Rhea. It's good of you to turn out like this.'

'All part of the service,' I smiled, and turned for home. I gave this incident no further thought – it was just one of many that day. The weather did not improve for almost a week. Severe snow-storms attacked our moorland communities and some isolated farmsteads had to have fodder carried in by helicopter to feed sheep trapped on the high moors. A pregnant woman, about to give birth, was airlifted to Strensford Maternity Home. But the local people were quite capable of surviving – in the run-up to any winter, all practical country folk lay in sufficient stocks of food and fuel for just such an eventuality and, apart from the inconvenience and cold of the period, no real harm was done.

It would be on the fourth or fifth day of that bout of extreme weather that Mary, my wife, returned from a shopping expedition in the village. With an air of one who knows, she said, 'Have you heard about Eileen Barton?'

'No, what's happened?' I wondered if she'd got trapped in a snowdrift or whether her smart new car had been involved in some kind of drama.

'She's changed all the locks on her house,' Mary said. 'Only this morning. She's locked Michael out.'

'Really?' I had no inkling there was any kind of marital trouble between the Bartons. They'd always seemed totally content with each other. 'What's happened?'

'Well,' said Mary, adopting the style of a woman about to impart an item or two of juicy gossip. 'Apparently, he's been seeing another woman for some time. Months, in fact, and Eileen became suspicious. She's been keeping an eye on him; I don't think he realized she knew what he was up to. He said he was working late a lot; he was taking long lunches, having time off and leaving the shop to the care of his assistants – the usual stuff. Anyway, when he said he was staying at the Black Swan in Ashfordly, during the blizzards, she rang them when the lines were restored – and they knew nothing about it. He'd been staying with his fancy piece – she's called Ann, she's divorced: she has a house in Ashfordly and works in the Rural District Council offices. Eileen has been preparing for this day – she bought a new set of door locks a few weeks ago, in readiness. Now she's done it – she's locked him out. I got all this from Hilary Hughes.'

'I always thought they were such a happy couple,' was all I could think of saying. 'There's been no hint of trouble, not to my knowledge.'

'You policemen aren't always completely aware of what's going on!' she smiled knowingly.

'So what happens next?' I asked.

'He's moving in with his new woman and Eileen's deciding what to do with her future,' Mary said. 'But he can't get into the house, she's locked him out. She threw his clothes into the garden, in all the snow, then told him.'

Sometimes in these cases, there is a blazing row, but with the Bartons it was all done very quietly. Michael went to work and Eileen didn't let him come back. It was as simple as that – although I am sure that, behind the scenes, there were pleadings, tears, apologies, regrets. . . .

It was about a month after the lock-out, when the snow had thawed and the roads no longer caused problems, that there was a knock on my office door. I opened it to find Eileen Barton standing there with a gentleman at her side. I invited them into my office, not knowing the reason for their visit.

'I'm sorry to involve you like this, PC Rhea,' apologized Eileen, 'but this gentlemen felt that an impartial witness was required for a transaction between us.'

'Something to sign?' I asked, for I was sometimes asked to witness applications for passports and such.

The man spoke. 'My name is James Ingram: I'm a businessman from Redcar. I saw this advert in the *Northern Echo* which is why I am here,' and he passed a small cutting to me. I took it. It was an advert in the For Sale columns for motor vehicles and read: *For Sale. Three-month-old Jaguar 3.4 saloon, red, 900 miles only from new. Genuine reason for sale. 7s. 6d. Also grandfather clock, circa 1809, keeps perfect time. 2s 6d.* This was followed by Eileen's address and telephone number.

I looked at Eileen, frowning at the price she was asking for these two expensive objects. The car was worth at least £1,500 and she was offering it for 7s. 6d. (37.5p in decimalized money); with the grandfather clock. also worth a considerable sum, the entire package could be obtained for ten shillings (50p).

'Do you mean this?' I asked her. 'You'll accept ten shillings for the car and the clock together?'

'It's not for me, it's for Michael,' she smiled, passing me a letter. Bearing an address in Ashfordly, it was addressed to Eileen and expressed deep regret for what he had done. Then it ended: *I can't get my Jaguar out of the garage and I need some cash urgently. Please sell the Jaguar and the grandfather clock and send me the money.*

Eileen explained, 'I am selling the items just as he has

instructed, but he does not tell me how much he wants for them.'

'What I want to know,' said Ingram, 'Is whether all this is legal! I thought it was a joke when I read the advert, but I rang to find out and was told it was a nearly new car . . . so I got here as fast as I could.'

'Very understandable!' I laughed.

'I can't believe my luck. I just want someone to witness all this, someone independent.'

'Well, I can witness what's transpired here and can't see anything illegal in it, Eileen. Michael has not given any indication of the price he requires; his instructions are quite specific and they are given in writing so, yes, I can't see either of you are committing any kind of crime. You have stated a price for the items and that price has been accepted – I am sure that is a legal contract although I wouldn't like to be categoric about all aspects of civil law. To be absolutely sure, it might be an idea for you to have words with a solicitor. But, from the criminal law side of things, there's no offence. I'm sure Michael will be delighted with his ten shillings!'

And so the deed was done, although prior to completing the deal, Eileen did have words with a solicitor who lived in Aidensfield. He expressed an opinion that the contract was quite lawful, and thus a wronged lady got part of her revenge without any physical bother. Michael lost his beloved Jaguar, his equally beloved grandfather clock and his beloved wife, a high penalty for his philandering. I have no idea how Michael and his new partner received this news, but things between them did not last. Oddly enough, Michael and Eileen were unhappy without each other and they were reunited a year or so later. Their shop, Bartons, was sold to a northern chain of hardware stores, whereupon Michael and Eileen bought a house in the Lake District where, I understand, they began a new life and lived happily ever after.

Some might argue that the penalties imposed by law for criminal offences are in themselves a form of group revenge while others would say they are merely a form of suitable punishment meted out by society. Punishment, properly administered, is not quite the same as personal revenge, however, but some victims of crime do feel that the punishment rarely compensates for the anguish and distress they have had to suffer. At times, personal revenge does seem to be an option. The topic of what constitutes suitable punishment has been argued down the centuries and there is no clear answer. It is no surprise, therefore, that some victims feel that the only way to deal with an offender, particularly one who avoids being caught, is to give him (or her) a taste of his own medicine. The law does not allow this kind of personal punishment, of course, but some victims, their friends and families do feel that justice has been done if an offender is well and truly taught a lesson without the courts or legal system knowing anything about it.

We had an example of that in Ashfordly.

Toby Hicks, aged 33, was a single man who lived with his widowed mother in a council house at 17, Scoresby Way, Ashfordly. A shop assistant in a department store at Ashfordly, Toby had long been suspected of stealing women's underwear from clothes lines in Ashfordly and possibly elsewhere. He specialized in knickers ignoring brassieres, stockings, tights and underslips. He removed his trophies during the hours of darkness and it seems he had no preference as regards age, colour or condition although he seemed to like fairly large pairs. The snag was that no one saw him steal the items and he was never caught with any in his possession.

He had been questioned many times about these thefts and, occasionally, subjected to a swift and unproductive search, but he always denied any responsibility. The only time he was arrested (because he was found near the scene of the crime within minutes of the victim raising the alarm), both he and his home were searched but no stolen goods were found. Although there was no positive evidence against him, I think it is fair to say that every police officer in the town suspected that Toby was the phantom knicker-nicker in spite of his denials. But no one had been able to prove it. Likewise, residents in the town, particularly those who had been victims of his peculiar collecting mania, also felt that he was the culprit and some of them could not understand why the police had never prosecuted him. It is difficult to explain the processes and limitations of criminal law to someone who will not listen or who does not try to understand – and who seems determined to take their own action to stem the crimes.

There was no pattern to Toby's crimes which meant we could not lay a trap for him or lie in wait at one of his projected visits. We had no idea where or when he was likely to strike next. He did not repeatedly venture forth at the same time or on the same night of the week; he did not stick to a particular area so far as target addresses were concerned and he did not restrict his activities to the clothes lines of ladies who were known to him. Because some of the victims left their washing on the line overnight, some of the losses were not noticed until breakfast-time next day and that made it difficult for us to know what time he was committing his crimes.

Others had recorded their losses before eleven in the evening, but we did know that all the crimes occurred in darkness. We were also sure that lots of knickers were stolen and never reported to us, probably due to the victims' embarrassment.

Married women, single women, old women and young women were all victims. If there was a common factor, it was perhaps that in every case the clothes were stolen from lines in back gardens well away from street lights and lounge windows, and they were gardens into which access could be gained from a rear lane, quiet footpath or dark alleyway. It was perhaps this mode of access to the gardens which told us that the thief was a local person with an intimate knowledge of the town's layout, but we did not think he targeted a particular victim. It was highly unlikely that he knew the name of any lady to whom his trophies belonged.

Although I was responsible for Aidensfield beat, I did patrol Ashfordly from time to time and it was through these visits that I became aware of Toby's activities. I was also shown Toby as he walked home one evening – my Ashfordly colleague, PC Alwyn Foxton, revealed the identity of the pasty-faced man who simpered across the market square. If I caught him red-handed, I would recognize him.

Those with civil liberties in mind might wonder how we could say that Toby was the knicker thief when we had never caught him in the act or found evidence upon him, but such knowledge comes from a combination of expert police intelligence, local knowledge, character assessment and snippets of corroborative evidence which are insufficient to persuade a court of a person's guilt, but enough to convince the police that further enquiries would be justified.

The practice is to build upon that foundation of initial knowledge to such an extent that a court of law can be convinced. The fact is we knew Toby was the thief. There was never any doubt about that. Our only problem was catching him and proving our suspicions to the satisfaction of a court of law. And for that we needed witnesses to say they had seen him stealing the underwear, we needed to catch him with some stolen goods in his possession and, if at all possible, we wanted a voluntary admission from him. The continuing absence of these ingredients suggested he was a very clever knicker-nicker.

Over the years, we had collated a considerable file about Toby and these crimes. In five years there were seventy such thefts, sixty of them within the town and ten in the neighbouring villages of Briggsby and Stovensby, both within walking distance of Ashfordly. None of the property was recovered. In twenty of the Ashfordly cases, Toby had been seen in the town on the evening in question, invariably within quarter of a mile of the attacked washing line. His practice appeared to be to leave home after supper, usually between 9 p.m. and 10 p.m., and go for what he called a breath of fresh air. He would walk around the town window shopping, but never popping into any of the pubs for a pint of beer, and he'd return around 11 p.m. He appeared to like walking alone in the darkness and his mother invariably waited up for him with a cup of cocoa.

We did maintain low-key observations on the house so we

could check his movements, but apart from determining these times, we learned little else, apart from the fact he led a very solitary and limited social life outside the house.

Of course, if he stole just one pair of pants at a time, which appeared to be his MO, then he could hide these about himself and a casual observer would never know he'd stolen or concealed them. The snag with keeping watch on the house was that we never knew if he'd stolen anything on the occasions we saw him because the victim herself would probably not know her washing line had been raided. Her discovery would be too late for us to effect a personal search of Toby – and in any case, our powers to stop and search a person without reasonable suspicion of a crime were somewhat limited. If no crime was reported at that particular time, we could do very little by way of searching Toby, and certainly we were not justified in searching him on the off-chance we would find something. We needed some kind of evidence or what is called 'reasonable suspicion' and we were aware that he went out of the house on many occasions without stealing knickers.

One thought did occur to me, however. When he had been searched, very soon after a theft had been reported, nothing was found on him or at his home, but I wondered just how thorough that search had been. Suppose, I thought to myself, he actually wore the pants that he stole; suppose he put them on within minutes of stealing them . . . the fact he selected fairly roomy bloomers added to my theory, but unless he was subjected to a strip search, the evidence would not be found. I made a mental note to impart my idea to Sergeant Blaketon should Toby ever be arrested in the future.

There is no doubt Toby's furtive activities unsettled and embarrassed the ladies of Ashfordly – and for that reason, it annoyed their husbands and boyfriends.

It came to our knowledge that two men, acting together, had stopped Toby during one of his night outings and had threatened him with a thumping if he persisted in his knicker raids, but if Toby had been frightened by their behaviour, it did not stop him. A week later, a pair of knickers vanished from a clothes line two streets away, and two days after that, another pair went from a line on a new housing estate. We were sure other lines were being raided without being reported to us and although we kept Toby under observation in an attempt to link him with any raids, we did not succeed. Toby went walkies and knickers went missing. We think that every time he stole a pair, he used a secret way back to his home, probably crossing fields and using a complicated unlit route known only to himself. Certainly there were nights he was never seen outside the house and yet knickers were stolen on those nights. I felt sure he knew we were keeping him under observation and that he enjoyed dodging our officers.

Our inability to catch him was highly frustrating and I knew that it led to a lot of criticism from the people of Ashfordly. Although we were as anxious as they to catch Toby, there were rules of procedure which had to be obeyed and so his one-man knicker campaign continued. But then the people literally took the law into their own hands. By chance, I was on duty in Ashfordly one Wednesday night in August. It was a hot, airless night with a threat of thunder and a full moon which bathed the town in its glow.

A young, well-built woman living in a house in the middle of Greenfinch Terrace went out moments before eleven o'clock to bring in her washing.

The back door had been standing open while she, her father, mother and two brothers were in the house. In silence, therefore, the girl walked into the garden to collect her things off the line and, to her horror, noticed a man near her washing. She'd shouted and he ran away. She screamed next and her family rushed to her assistance as the fellow, a dark anonymous character in the moonlight, leapt a dividing fence and then galloped headlong down the dark lane behind the terrace. Her menfolk gave chase – and they knew the area sufficiently well to cut off any flight by such a person and so the men had split into three to head off their prey. The girl, in the meantime, checked her washing to find a pair of black silk knickers had vanished. A search of the garden and lane immediately outside failed to trace them.

In the meantime, the thief had vanished too. He managed to conceal himself in the shadows of the moonlight and quickly went to ground among the conglomeration of garden sheds, greenhouses, dustbins, outbuildings and shrubs, clearly content to wait until the men called off their hunt. But they had no intention of calling it off . . . they knew he must be somewhere close and so they waited too, most determined to catch and identify the thief.

They did catch him. As Toby emerged from his hiding place under cover of the extra darkness created by a cloud obscuring the moon, the men pounced on him. Toby did his best to retaliate but stood little chance against the might of the three stalwarts. After identifying him, they beat him mercilessly about the body and head, then abandoned him.

Toby, semi-conscious by this stage, staggered along the lane and emerged onto a quiet road where he was seen in the lights of a passing car. The driver happened to be an off-duty ambulanceman. He stopped, assessed the battered condition of Toby within seconds, and whisked him off to Strensford Hospital, leaving him in casualty as an in-patient. Having ascertained his name and address, the hospital authorities rang Ashfordly Police Station because the attack constituted a serious crime – assault occasioning actual bodily harm at the very least – and they felt we should be informed.

As I was on duty that night, I took the call. The moment I was given the name of the victim, I guessed he had been beaten up by someone who'd caught him nicking knickers. It was probably not the first time that had happened but first there was the humane aspect of the case to consider. I asked the caller if the patient wanted his mother or any relatives or friends informed of his hospitalization. My contact was the ward sister and she told me the patient had declined – he said he'd ring his mother himself, from the hospital pay-phone.

Then, after establishing that Toby was fit to be interviewed, I decided to drive to Strensford Hospital for a chat with him. When I arrived, I was shown him through a window of the side ward where he lay. With dressings on his face, arms and head, he was lying in bed wearing hospital pyjamas and looked a pathetic sight.

'He's had a thorough beating, a really tough and sustained battering with fists and feet,' the ward sister explained. 'But he won't tell us what happened or say who did it.'

'Did you undress him?' I asked eventually.

'We did,' she smiled, as if anticipating my next question.

'Was he wearing a pair of woman's knickers?'

'Yes, he was,' she grinned. 'Black silk ones, quite nice actually.'

'Now you know why he was attacked,' and I told her about the phantom knicker-nicker of Ashfordly. At that stage I had no idea where or when Toby had obtained those particular knickers, but I felt I now knew where he usually concealed his freshly stolen trophies: he wore them. In some respects, he must have been a quick-change expert, but it was a good means of avoiding detection even if he was searched. Who would think of searching beneath his clothing for such things? The next task was to interview him in the hope I could obtain an admission or explanation.

When I walked into his ward, in full uniform, his bruised features hardened and I knew I faced a difficult task.

'Toby Hicks?' I began.

'Yes,' he said, turning his eyes away from me as I settled on a chair at his side. I gave my own name and explained that the hospital had called the police due to his injuries, then asked again whether he wanted me to inform his mother or anyone else. He shook his head.

'I'll do it, when I'm ready,' he muttered. 'They'll let me out soon, so they said.'

'You know why I am here?' I put to him.

'Because I got beat up,' he said. 'But it's no good asking me, I have no idea who they were or why they did this to me.'

'Did they steal anything?' I asked.

'Money, you mean? No, nothing. They just thumped and kicked me, then ran away.'

'Where was the attack?' I asked.

'The back lane, just behind Greenfinch Terrace,' he said.

'What time?' was my next question.

'I dunno, not exactly. Half past ten maybe.'

'It was dark, then?'

'Yes, but there was a moon. It wasn't completely dark.'

'So what were you doing there?' I put to him.

'Walking, just walking. There's no law against that. Getting fresh air, away from the busy streets. Lots of people walk along that lane, Mr Rhea. I wasn't doing anything wrong.'

'I am not suggesting you were. I am just interested from a professional point of view. I will make sure I patrol that lane more diligently in the future. We don't want it to become known as a place where people can be attacked. Now, the attackers. How many were there?'

'Three or four, I can't be sure.'

'And who were they, Toby?'

'No idea,' he said.

'Can you describe them?'

'No, I can't. It was dark....'

'I think you might have some idea who they were.' I decided to press him on this issue.

'Look, I've no idea. No idea at all. Just three men, or four, I'm not even sure about that. I want nothing doing about this, and I don't want my mother told what's happened ... so can we just leave it, forget it....'

'An assault of this gravity is a serious matter,' I said. 'If you wish to make a formal complaint....'

'I don't,' he snapped. 'Forget it, can't you? I want nothing done, nothing at all. I will never be a witness against my attackers, that's if they are ever found, so there's no case, PC Rhea. No case at all.'

'But there might be a case of larceny, Toby, the stealing of women's underwear from clothes lines. You know there's been a long-running series of such thefts in Ashfordly because you have been interviewed many times. Now, I know you were wearing women's knickers when you arrived here, black silk ones. I wonder where you got them? And I wonder if you got chased away by the loser's husband or boyfriend or father....'

'I am saying nothing about that. There is no law to say a man cannot wear whatever he wants, PC Rhea. If I want to wear women's silk underwear, then there is nothing to stop me.'

'Right – except that it's a crime to steal them.'

'Then you prove they were stolen!'

I guessed, and he knew, that the girl who'd lost this particular pair would never complain because it would implicate her menfolk or friends if they were involved in the beating-up of Toby Hicks. In spite of my endeavours, Toby refused to describe his attackers, he would not admit any thefts of ladies' knickers and so, once again, we were unable to proceed against him. Afterwards, we never did prove the pants he wore that night had been stolen because no one came forward to report the theft.

Toby returned home later the following day, but, meanwhile, the town had heard of the attack upon him. I think his assailants had quietly spread the news that they'd caught him stealing from the clothes line and made sure everyone knew the identity of the knicker-nicker. However, no one admitted the assault upon him and due to his refusal to make a formal complaint, we could not press proceedings nor even make official enquiries.

But Toby received a further punishment for his crimes because the local children began to sing the rhyme:

'Toby Hicks, Toby Hicks, gets his kicks from ladies' knicks.'

His mother died within a few months of that incident, after which we learned from a friend that she had always known of Toby's fetish. Whenever Toby returned home with women's knickers, she would discover them in his bedroom and throw them into the dustbin. That prompted him to go out and steal another pair.

Soon after her death, Toby moved to Middlesbrough where he secured a post in yet another department store, this time as deputy manager of the clothing section.

His new responsibilities included lingerie and so he could indulge in his passion without fear, buying his undies during the course of his work instead of having to steal them.

With his departure, the Ashfordly knicker thefts came to an end but I must admit I wondered why, if he worked in a department store at Ashfordly, he never bought his special pants there instead of risking so much by stealing them. If the purchases embarrassed him, he could always have told staff members he was buying them for his mother – unless, of course, she preferred men's undergarments.

4

And thou shalt have none to rescue them.
Deuteronomy 28.31

Properly organized and equipped search and rescue teams which respond to people lost or hurt on the moors or mountains were a fairly recent innovation during my time at Aidensfield. Prior to their creation, people lost or injured on the North York Moors had to depend upon the skills of the local police forces or fire brigades with or without a host of valuable volunteers. Volunteers who did turn out ranged from the Territorial Army to the Boy Scouts by way of helpers from the nearest village or those who offered their services when the rescue attempt extended over a long period accompanied by lots of publicity.

I think it's fair to say they did a good job because most rescues were successful, whether they comprised a hiker with a broken leg or someone who had got lost either in a fog or through being unable to understand their map – if they'd taken the trouble to carry one. It was amazing how many people embarked on long expeditions in hostile country without a map, and lots did not wear suitable shoes or clothing nor did they carry food or drinks. As a consequence, a lot of numbskulls had to be rescued.

In time, of course, formal search and rescue organizations were established complete with radios, modern equipment and highly trained members. The emergency services – fire, police and ambulance – worked closely with them and their creation coincided with the increased leisure enjoyed by the great British public.

Increased leisure with a corresponding increase in the ownership of motor cars meant that larger numbers of visitors flocked to remote and mountainous areas of this country, one of which was the North York Moors. It was by then designated a National Park, but a lot of people seemed to think it was a town-like park with paddling pools, swings and roundabouts, and birds in cages. It was astonishing how many had no idea that this National Park was a huge wild piece of England with rivers, lakes, moorland heights, dales, a coastline and everything that such a beautiful landscape can contain, like castles, abbeys, pretty villages – and people who actually work and live there.

One effect of this expansion of leisure time and the facilities to enjoy it was that more people drove into the countryside from the towns and cities which in turn meant there were more people to get lost or injured – which they did with predictable frequency. At times, the fledgling search and rescue services were hard-pressed to keep pace with the demands placed upon them, and it is sad to record that lots of hours were wasted looking for people who were either ill-prepared for the task they wished to undertake, or who were never really lost. We had to contend with instances where foolish people told friends they were taking a particular route and who then took a different one while obtaining overnight accommodation instead of going home. They made these changes without informing their friends and families who, when their pals did not return at the appointed time, naturally thought they were lost or injured.

Many a search has been conducted in blizzards and dangerously hostile conditions while the object of the search was sitting in a pub over a log fire with a pint in his hands. There has long been a suggestion that idiots and fools whose actions result in a call-out should pay the bills incurred by the rescue services. I would subscribe to that.

Genuine calls for assistance were never criticized and it was through a succession of injuries and persons getting lost in fogs or blizzards that the Ashfordly Search and Rescue Organization was formed. It was inevitably known by its initials – ASRO – and comprised a volunteer force of men and women with the necessary local rural knowledge combined with fitness, rescue skills and bags of common sense. They included mountaineers, hikers, ex-military types, Forestry Commission workers, gamekeepers, doctors, nurses, police officers and others who would respond to emergencies if and when they arose. The secretary was Mrs Gillian Wetherby, an efficient and very charming woman in her thirties who was employed by the National Park Authority; she could be contacted at her office during the working day, and at home during the weekends and evenings. She had established an early-warning telephone system where one of her members on call rang three others when a call-out occurred, thus enabling a large group to assemble within a very short time. Fortunately, the National Park offices were spacious enough for a spare room to be set aside for accommodation of ASRO's equipment. ASRO was fortunate to have a base in such a place and in an area which was central for most of the searches.

Usually, it was the police, ambulance or fire brigade who initiated the call-outs after establishing, wherever possible, that a call was genuine. Sometimes, though, a person would make direct contact with ASRO, consequently the police or other emergency services were not necessarily involved with every call-out. And sometimes those calls produced interesting and curious results.

One of the early requests to ASRO came direct from a member of the public instead of through the emergency services. It happened on a hot August day when the moorland about us was bathed in shimmering heat. A well-spoken, middle-aged woman called Frances Piper staggered into a lonely farm on the moors wanting urgent help for her aged and exhausted companion. Her female companion had collapsed in the overpowering heat and could walk no further. Miss Piper arrived to find that the only occupant of the farm was a very elderly lady in a wheelchair. The other family members were harvesting nearly two miles away and so Miss Piper asked if she could use the telephone to summon help.

Fortunately, the farm in question, High Dale House at

Briggsby, had a list of emergency numbers pinned to the wall above the telephone. They included vets, doctors, nurses, shops, garages, and among them was the number of the recently formed Ashfordly Search and Rescue Organization. It was included because lost people often called at the remote farm seeking help. Quite understandably, Miss Piper rang ASRO and Gillian Wetherby responded. I was later given an account of this rescue by Gillian, hence my knowledge of events.

According to Gillian, Miss Piper, in tears, had rung to say her ageing companion, Mrs Robinson, had become totally exhausted in the heat. There was no shelter on the exposed moors and she could go no further; bravely, she had walked until she had dropped from sheer exhaustion. Miss Piper had managed to find a beck from which a drink of cool water had been obtained for Mrs Robinson, and then Miss Piper, a 62-year-old spinster from Huddersfield, had ordered her distressed companion to stay where she was until help arrived. Miss Piper had managed to find High Dale House from which to call for help. In responding to this call, Gillian Wetherby was aware of the dangers that could result from untreated sunstroke and heat exhaustion and realized she must act quickly. She asked for specific directions to the scene and managed to obtain a map reference which would take her volunteers straight to the casualty.

Then she set about recruiting sufficient volunteers to reach the casualty and, if necessary, to carry her on a stretcher to a waiting vehicle. The rescue effort entailed a five-mile trek by Land-rover from Ashfordly to the farm, followed by the walk of a mile across rough moorland to the casualty's resting place. Time was vital, but the moorland walk through difficult terrain and in intense heat would be arduous and tiring, even for fit people. Gillian knew there would be an even tougher walk on the return journey because they'd be bearing a loaded stretcher.

The ambulance service was alerted too, just in case more expert medical attention was needed, and they said they would rendezvous with ASRO at High Dale House.

And so the rescue attempt began with Gillian Wetherby going to the scene as one of the party.

'It was a blistering hot day on those moors,' she told me afterwards. 'Five of us trekked from the farm to the spot she'd identified and we soon found Miss Piper. She was waving a large white handkerchief to direct us, and she shouted that Mrs Robinson was still lying exhausted in a small gully just above High Gill. We ran to the scene with the stretcher and found her with no trouble. But you'll never guess who Mrs Robinson was!'

I knew that the rescue of a famous person was always good for such an organization because the subsequent publicity served both to warn the public of the dangers and to highlight the work of the search and rescue parties. But I shook my head – I could not think who Mrs Robinson might be; I considered it might be the real name of a pop star, the name of a faded musical-hall artist or film star, a person high in the professional world or politics or the arts. . . .

'Sorry, Gillian,' I had to admit. 'I've no idea who Mrs Robinson is.'

'She's a dog,' said Gillian. 'A great, fat, idle, golden labrador, far overweight and totally out of condition . . . she simply gave up in the heat and refused to move.'

'She called you out for a dog?' I cried. 'I don't believe it!'

'She did. The silly old woman . . . she had no thought to the fact we might be needed for a human being who'd collapsed or in dire straits.'

'So what did you do?'

She smiled. 'Our men took the stretcher to the dog, lifted it aboard and then took it to the gill. Then they dumped the dog in the cool water. It recovered immediately in spite of its age. It was fifteen years old, a big age for a dog.'

'And you'll send the silly Miss Piper a bill?'

'No, we can't really do that. It might be argued we should have carried out closer checks before responding, but we suggested she gave a useful donation to the team and sent a letter of apology to the ambulance service.'

'And did she?'

'As a matter of fact, yes. We got a hundred pounds from her. After all, we had cured the dog and it walked to the Land-rover with us! It was not a wasted day, though, we could consider the outing as a good training exercise, which it was. We learned lessons from it. And I'm sure we helped poor old Mrs Robinson.'

'Mrs Robinson, eh? An odd name for a dog,' I mused.

'When Miss Piper was working – she was a secretary in a clothing factory – she hated to say she had to rush home from social events or even from work, just to feed her dog. So she called the dog Mrs Robinson, so when she said she had to rush home to care for Mrs Robinson, no one argued or thought it odd. Not a bad idea, actually, and once we got to know her, she was quite a nice old lady.'

'Who? Mrs Robinson or the other one?' I laughed.

'Both,' she said.

The lessons learned from the rescue of Mrs Robinson were rapidly put into practice because, within a week, there was a second request for the services of the Ashfordly Search and Rescue Organization to go to the aid of a sick dog. On that occasion, it was rapidly established that the casualty was a dog and so ASRO turned down the request. As things worked out, Gillian, the ASRO secretary, was on holiday at the time and, during her absence, it had been decided by team members that all requests for ASRO's services should be directed through Ashfordly Police Station. It was one of the few places in the small market town which operated on a twenty-four-hour basis, and the local police were well equipped to implement the search and rescue procedures.

Although the call was taken by PC Alf Ventress, the decision not to turn out the ASRO team on that occasion was taken very speedily by Sergeant Blaketon who happened to be in the office at the time. I wondered if his decision was influenced in any way by the fact that the ailing dog was none other than Alfred, the scruffy lurcher, the best friend of Claude Jeremiah Greengrass. Quite by chance and rather unwittingly, I was later to become involved in that sick-dog saga, but the preamble happened like this.

For reasons known only to himself and perhaps to Alfred, Claude Jeremiah Greengrass was wandering across the loftiest parts of the North York Moors. It was a hot August day, the heather was in full bloom and the moors, at their most spectacular during the latter weeks of that month, were a sea of incredible purple plants, millions of them.

I don't think Claude was there to admire the scenery, however. The fact that the grouse shooting season had been underway since the Glorious Twelfth might have had some bearing on his presence that day although, in his usual manner, he steadfastly denied being on the moors for nefarious purposes. Nonetheless, he was in possession of a twelve bore shotgun and cartridges at the time, and Alfred was searching the heather and periodically putting up birds. I cannot say whether Greengrass succeeded in bagging a brace or two because he never admitted such a thing, nor did I, when I became involved, find him in possession of any shot grouse. On the other hand, he did not have any transport and I wondered if he'd secreted it somewhere until the coast was clear.

However, it seems that Alfred, busy snuffling through the thick, strong heather, failed to see an adder which was basking on a patch of dry, bare earth. The adder is Britain's only poisonous snake. Growing to a length of two feet in the case of the male, and up to two feet six inches so far as females are concerned, these handsome creatures can be identified by the black zig-zag or diamond-shaped markings which run the length of their spines. Their base colour can vary from a warm, light brown to a dark grey colour but in general they are docile creatures which will not attack without reason. At the approach of danger, they much prefer to slide away and disappear in the undergrowth, but if challenged they can adminster a nasty bite which injects poisonous venom into their adversary. In this case, Alfred arrived quickly on the scene without the dozing adder being aware of his proximity, and, snuffling through the heather, he had nudged the snake from its slumbers.

Reacting instinctively, it bit its foe – it seized Alfred by his lower lip. The dog howled and threw up his head in surprise and pain, at which Claude saw the snake being thrown over Alfred's back as it released its grip. It sailed across the heather for a few feet and then crashed to earth to disappear among the deep plants. Observing this little drama, Claude knew what had happened. He knew that the bite of an adder was rarely fatal in humans, unless they were allergic to the venom, but he had no idea of its effect upon dogs. He was soon to learn.

The immediate effect seemed to be nil and apart from constantly licking the wound, Alfred did not appear to be seriously injured, but within half an hour, he was struggling to walk and a few minutes later collapsed in a heap. He appeared to be in a coma and, despite entreaties from Claude, failed to respond. Claude, extremely upset at the thought of Alfred dying, picked up the dog in his arms and hurried for help. On those exposed wastes, however, there were no houses, farms or telephone kiosks and it took him nearly an hour to reach the moorland hamlet of Lairsbeck. By this stage, Claude was almost walking on all fours through exhaustion; sweat was pouring from him and his old legs were aching interminably. Alfred had made no progress, but happily he was still alive, his thin chest showing that his heart continued to beat.

There is a roadside telephone kiosk in Lairsdale and Claude had just enough money to make a couple of calls. Luckily, someone had written the number of the Ashfordly Search and Rescue Organization in the kiosk, a wise idea in this remote dale, and so Claude rang them.

But, as we know, Gillian was on holiday and the person deputizing for her in the National Park office, told Claude to ring the police who would make arrangements for the call-out. With his last coin, Claude did so. After first talking to Alf Ventress, Sergeant Blaketon took over and immediately turned down his request. Thus Claude was marooned in Lairsdale with no money, no vehicle, his twelve bore and a very sick Alfred. Almost weeping with dejection, he sat on the ground outside the kiosk, laid the gun on the ground and cradled Alfred in his arms. He would wait in the hope that a Good Samaritan might pass this way. There was nothing else he could do.

It was at that stage that the radio in my Mini-van came to life and I heard my call sign being broadcast. I was patrolling the hills, dales and villages around Brantsford and received a loud and clear signal.

'It's Alf Ventress,' said the distinctive voice. 'What's your location, Nick?'

'Brantsford area, Alf, approaching Rannockdale,' I responded.

'Look,' said Alf, reducing his voice until I could hardly hear him, 'Sergeant Blaketon's popped into town for half an hour, so I thought I'd call you while he's out of the way. We got a call from Greengrass; he rang from the kiosk in Lairsdale. He's in a bit of state, his dog is ill with a snake bite, he tried to get ASRO to go out and help him but Blaketon wouldn't sanction it, not for a dog. Claude hasn't got his pick-up truck or any transport. I wondered if you were anywhere near Lairsdale, just to see if we can do anything to help the poor old rogue get his dog seen to.'

'I can be there in twenty minutes,' I said. 'I'll see what I can do.'

'Well done, Nick. Not a word to Blaketon. If he asks, you were just passing and you happened to come across Claude!'

'Right. Now, those kiosks take incoming calls so can you ring Claude and tell him to wait for me? Twenty minutes or so.'

When I arrived, Claude was still sitting on the ground nursing Alfred and the relief on his face as I pulled up was a joy to behold. He gabbled the story to me as I urged him to put the dog and gun in the rear and then get into the front passenger seat beside me, but Claude refused. He wanted to nurse Alfred, and so both of them squeezed into the cramped front seat of the Mini as I laid his gun in the rear, checking that it was unloaded. Then I turned around and drove off.

'You'll get it in the neck, Constable Nick, for using police transport to come and give my dog a lift.'

'Look, if anybody asks, I happened to be on patrol in

Lairsdale and found you and Alfred in a distressed condition. Right? And if Blaketon sees us, you'd better have a licence for that gun!'

'Anything you say, Constable! And I do have a gun licence. Anyroad, where are you taking us?'

'To the vet in Harrowby, it's not far out of my way,' I said. 'If Alfred's been bitten by an adder, he needs treatment.'

I dropped Claude, Alfred and the gun at the vet's surgery in Harrowby, but Claude advised me not to wait. He said he would find his own way home because he wanted to take sufficient time to ensure Alfred was properly treated.

As I left, he said he'd leave a couple of pints for me at the Hopbind Inn next time I called, his way of expressing his gratitude.

As there were a further two hours to my patrol before I knocked off duty, I decided to head for Eltering, there to execute a foot patrol of the town centre, visit a few villages and farms, and head back to Aidensfield to knock off at 6 p.m. At two minutes to six, as I turned down the road which led to my police house, I noticed Sergeant Blaketon's car parked outside. He was there to book me off duty, to make sure I did not sneak into the house before the end of my shift.

'All correct, Rhea?' he asked, as I clambered out of the Minivan to meet him.

'Yes, Sergeant. No problems. I've done an extended patrol of the Brantsford areas and Eltering town centre. All's very quiet.'

'We were nearly made busy with an ASRO call-out,' he smiled. 'We could have been dragged into a search and rescue operation on the moors but I smelt a rat – or to be precise, a rather mucky dog. It was Greengrass, would you believe, ringing the ASRO headquarters and wanting them to go out and bring his dog home. I dread to think what might have happened if I'd not taken the call . . . we'd be the laughing stock of the area, rushing off to rescue sick dogs! And now, would you believe, I was in your village centre a few minutes ago and there was Greengrass with his dog and gun, as large as life, getting off Arnold Merryweather's bus! Sick dog my foot! He'd been shooting and that mutt of his was as fit as a lop. You've got to keep one step ahead of Greengrass, Rhea. Next thing we know, folks will be wanting search and rescue parties to clean up after their picnics or fetch the hamper back to base.'

'Yes, Sergeant,' I nodded, recalling an incident where a search and rescue party was asked to ferry people down from the moors because otherwise they'd be late for a dinner party. That request was turned down. 'It would have been a very hot job, searching those moors in this heat.'

'It would indeed. Well, Rhea, another peaceful and uneventful day. Get yourself booked off duty. I'll see you tomorrow – and make sure Greengrass has a licence for that gun of his.'

'Very good, Sergeant,' I smiled as he drove away.

I was delighted that Alfred was all right and thought a couple of pints of cool refreshing beer, paid for by Claude, would be a very good reason for popping into the pub on this hot, August evening.

The Ashfordly Search and Rescue team did have more serious work to consider and a good example occurred one year in the week after August Bank Holiday Monday, which at that time was the first Monday in August. This was the time for school holidays and some Girl Guides came to camp on a site close to a moorland stream which flows past Hagg Bottom. Hagg Bottom is the location of the Greengrass ranch but their campsite was not on Claude's property. It was only a couple of fields away, however, at a place known as Hagg Carr which was regularly used to accommodate Scout and Guide camps. Claude regarded this as a most convenient arrangement because he offered to supply, for a price, of course, fresh eggs and goat milk or anything else they might require.

His range of merchandise included frying pans, bundles of firewood, tent pegs, paraffin, candles and even extra food such as sausages, potatoes and tins of baked beans.

This particular group of Guides came from Leeds. They were known as the Seventh Woodhouse (Leeds) Girl Guides and comprised some two dozen teenage girls aged between eleven and fifteen. They were led by a busy and efficient Guider called Sylvia McNeil who was in her late thirties and whose 14-year-old daughter, Susan, was one of the campers. The girls arrived on the Friday before Bank Holiday Monday and the camp was to continue until a week the following Saturday, nine days in total. Some of the girls arrived in cars which the Guiders drove and others travelled from their homes military style in the back of a covered lorry which also transported their tents, food, sleeping-bags and other gear. A couple of mothers accompanied the troop to help Sylvia in her work, and the lorry driver, the father of another of the girls, helped them unload and erect their tents. Once the camp-fire was burning, the tents erected, the evening meal under way and the girls unpacked, they had a sing-song around the blazing log fire as a means of blending them into one cohesive unit prior to their first night under canvas.

In general, the police service was not concerned with or worried about Scouts and Guides who came to camp in their area, although in the case of a small village it was usually wise for the resident constable to acquaint himself with such arrivals. Almost invariably, the camps were well supervised by responsible leaders and their young charges were well behaved.

Sadly, there were a few instances where undisciplined Scouts or Guides from inner-city areas escaped into the nearest village to shoplift sweets or steal apples and fruit from the local store or even from cottage gardens. In Aidensfield, such cases were very rare indeed and we seldom experienced problems from Guides and Scouts. Sometimes, of course, snoopers and peepers would prowl the vicinity of the camp-site under cover of darkness, particularly if interesting female campers were likely to be observed; consequently, it was wise for a police uniform to be evident at some stage of the campers' stay. For that reason, I would patrol the vicinity of the camps from time to time, hoping my uniform would serve as a deterrent to wrongdoers.

In the case of this group, I was aware of their arrival because Joe Steel, the owner of the village shop, informed me. He'd been contacted in advance to supply some grocery items, and he'd put

Sylvia in touch with the milkman and local butcher. In that typically village way, most of the population of Aidensfield was soon aware that a troop of Girl Guides from Leeds was camping close to the Greengrass estate.

I always made a point of calling at such camps soon after their arrival so that those in charge knew me and my address, should they require my aid in any emergency, large or small. I was amazed at some of the things that happened during these modest camping holidays. In the short time I had been at Aidensfield, the following calamities had happened to a succession of campers – tents had caught fire; campers had broken arms, legs and ankles or burned their fingers, got stung with wasps or cut with broken glass in the river; some campers had been flooded while asleep at night when the river rose unexpectedly; cattle had broken out of a field and trampled the tents while the campers were away for the day, vehicles had broken down or refused to start; foxes had raided the larders . . . these were among a variety of relatively minor incidents during just a few summers and it was all part of the fun.

I must admit that when the Seventh Woodhouse Guides arrived, I wondered whether we would experience any memorable incidents. I paid my usual visit to the site, met the leaders and wished them a happy stay in Aidensfield but other than noticing the Guides in and around the village during the first few days, there were no incidents of concern to me. Wednesday, however, was adventure day. The entire troop was divided into its various patrols, each supervised by its own patrol leader. They had to equip themselves for a long day walking in the woods and on the moors, including the preparation of the ingredients for a meal they would take with them to cook during their outing. The objective was to find their way to a given point – in this case the Hermit's Cave in Ghylldale – and then return to the camp by using a simple map. Along the route would be a series of challenges and adventures, such as lighting fires with natural materials to cook their meals, measuring the height of trees, identifying birds, animals and plants seen *en route*, finding their way by using a map, compass and natural features, seeing which patrol could find and identify the most kinds of fungi, crossing streams by building bridges or making stepping stones and then writing up the entire exercise, with drawings where appropriate. A spirit of competition was introduced by challenging each patrol to bring back the most species of tree leaves, all correctly identified, and to sketch all the different types of stile they crossed during the day.

Outings of this kind were hugely popular and by ten that bright and sunny morning, the excited girls were heading for the hills. They returned tired and happy, all with interesting tales to tell and it was the Woodpecker Patrol, led by 14-year-old Susan McNeil which emerged winner of the day's competition. Its members were each given a small certificate to record their success and after an evening meal, the youngsters went to bed early, some of them very tired indeed.

Next morning, Thursday, Susan was missing. When the other girls in her tent awoke, they noticed the empty sleeping-bag but initially were not concerned. Susan usually woke first and went outside for a wash and to the toilet, then set about rousing the others. In this, she was a good patrol leader, caring for the others, helping them where necessary, but ensuring that all obeyed the rules of the camp. But when her Second, Ann Knowles, also fourteen, went to find her, Susan was nowhere to be seen. Ann, slightly concerned, went to tell Susan's mother, Sylvia.

Together, Sylvia and Ann made a search of the camp-site, examining all the places likely to have been visited bv Susan, including the other tents on the site, but she was nowhere to be seen. The other girls were roused and asked if they'd seen her but none had. Some thought she might have popped into Aidensfield to get some breakfast provisions from the shop and so they waited for half an hour, just in case, but Susan did not return. One of the adult helpers drove into the village in her own car to make a brief search, but there was no sign of Susan. By this stage, almost an hour had passed with no indication of her whereabouts. She had not left a note to explain her absence, nor had she told anyone else where she was going.

It was then that an increasingly worried Sylvia McNeil hurried to my house and knocked on the door. It was 8.30 and I was already up and dressed. I took her into my office and Mary produced a cup of fresh tea from our breakfast pot. After listening to Sylvia's account of events up to that point, including Susan's role as patrol leader for yesterday's adventure day, I asked, 'So what is she wearing?'

'Oh, I've no idea, Mr Rhea,' she admitted. 'Is that important?'

'Well, it would be useful to know if she's wearing her nightclothes or her day clothes, her Guide uniform, for example? I have to consider whether she's gone voluntarily, perhaps just taking an early morning walk or exploring, or whether we have to consider something more disturbing.'

'Oh, I see. Sorry, I didn't check her bedspace.'

'I need to know so I'll come to the camp with you,' I said, and within minutes was heading for Hagg Bottom. I drove the short distance in my Mini-van while Sylvia returned to the site in the car she had borrowed. When I entered the camp-site, I saw the girls were hanging around in small groups, talking among themselves in low voices and there was a prevailing air of bleak anticipation. During Sylvia's absence, word of Susan's disappearance had reached everyone and although a careful search of the site had been made, no sign of Susan had been found.

It took a few moments to establish she had dressed herself in her Guide uniform, a blue dress with the patrol leader's insignia, along with blue socks and black shoes.

And she had been in her bed at eleven o'clock last night, when Svlvia made her final rounds. Her toothbrush, soap, face cloth and other toiletries were in her holdall and so it seemed she had not left the site with the intention of remaining away for long. I suggested a telephone call to her home address, just to check whether she had made her way home for any reason. Not knowing what time she had left the site, she might have had time to reach Leeds by bus or rail. Sylvia said she would do that – her husband, Ray, would be at home this week, doing some decorating. As Sylvia drove once again into the village to the telephone kiosk, I conducted a very thorough search of the camp-site, examining every tent, vehicle, boot of vehicle, food store, toilets and even an old derelict building, but I found no trace of the missing girl and no evidence to suggest a reason for her absence.

Throughout these necessary exercises, however, time was passing – and as time passed with no sign of Susan, my concern (and the concern of her mother and friends) was increasing. I was rapidly approaching the moment when I had to decide whether to extend and expand the search because when a young girl is missing from her usual haunts, there can often be sinister reasons. The alternative was to continue as if it was little more than the case of a senior schoolgirl who was late home from a morning walk. Teenagers were often late home for a variety of reasons. At this stage, there was no evidence to suggest Susan had been forcibly removed from her bed or that she had been the victim of a sexual attack or assault of any kind, serious or minor.

Although, in the nature of my work, I had not to lose sight of the fact she might have become the victim of a sex attacker, I had likewise to balance the facts with the possibility she had gone for a morning walk or possibly that she had had an early morning liaison with a boyfriend. Again, there was no evidence to suggest such a meeting, but these things are not impossible, even during Girl Guide camping weeks. All the available evidence, particularly the fact she had taken the time to dress in her uniform, suggested she had risen early from her bed to go for a walk – and had simply failed to return.

If that was the case, was she late because she had misjudged the distance and time involved in her walk, or had she injured herself? As I searched the shores of the river which flowed past the site, I was trying to make up my mind about the next stage of my action. Meanwhile, Sylvia returned from telephoning home to say her husband, Ray, had had no messages from Susan, nor had she arrived at her Leeds home. He decided to remain in the house in case she did return for any reason – but he asked his wife to keep in regular contact with home, not an easy task with a telephone kiosk as one's only line of contact.

Before deciding whether to expand the search, I called all the Guides and Guiders together because I wanted to quiz them all about Susan. I felt this was the best way, rather than conduct individual interrogations of all the campers. I asked them to gather in front of a chair upon which I would stand to address them. As they were ushered into a quiet group before me, I climbed onto the chair and began.

'My name is PC Rhea,' I introduced myself by name. 'I am the village constable here in Aidensfield as some of you already know, and I live in the police house. Now, you know why I am here. Susan has disappeared; all of you know her and she is dressed in her Guide uniform. She was in bed last night, we know that, but this morning when Ann, her Second, went to look for her, she had vanished. We don't know what time she got out of bed which means we have no idea how long she has been missing, how far she might have gone – or where she might have gone. I don't think she has been kidnapped or anything nasty like that because she got dressed in her uniform. I think she might have gone for a walk and either got lost or perhaps injured herself. The question now is: what can we do to find her? I think the first fact I have to establish is whether anything has happened which might make her want to go off alone.'

At that stage, I paused for a moment to allow my words to have their effect, and then continued, 'Now you've all been with her for the past few days, living together, talking among yourselves, having the adventure day yesterday, that sort of thing. So, can anyone give me any idea why Susan might have wanted to get up early this morning and go off to be all by herself?'

I paused for a second time, now scanning the faces grouped before me in the hope that one of them might produce some clue or hint which could be followed up but no one said anything. The Guides, clearly frightened to some degree, merely stood and gazed up at me. I knew the difficulties in talking to children, but some of these were fairly mature young women.

'If Susan said anything, anything at all, please tell the policeman,' Sylvia urged them, speaking both as a mother and as the Guider in charge.

As I stood and faced this silent group, I noticed two girls nudging Ann Knowles, the guide who had raised the alarm. They were whispering to her and I saw their actions even though they were in the midst of the crowd.

'Ann,' I asked her direct, 'is there something we should know?'

Ann, looking nervous in case she was going to get herself into trouble, hesitated, but the others encouraged her to talk and she said, 'Well, sir, yesterday, on the adventure day, we came to a waterfall. We had to cross the stream, sir; there was a bridge further up. But when we got to the waterfall. . . .' And at that stage, she halted in her narrative.

'And who is "we"?' I interrupted her, smiling to give her encouragement to continue.

'The Woodpecker patrol, sir, when we were map reading.'

'Ah, I see. Go on, Ann,' I hoped my relaxed attitude would be encouraging. 'You got to the waterfall, then what?'

'Well, there was a tree trunk lying across the water, sir, a big one, right near the top of the waterfall. It was an old rotten tree, lying right across from bank to bank, just like a bridge. We said we could use it to take a short cut, so we could get back to base first.'

'A short cut?' I puzzled.

'Yes, sir. The map said we should go further up the stream to a footbridge, but we worked out that if we crossed it on that tree trunk, we could save nearly a mile and get back to camp first. We said it would show what a good patrol the Woodpeckers were.'

'I can see what you mean,' I laughed. 'So did you cross by the old tree trunk?'

'No, sir, Susan wouldn't let us.'

'And why wouldn't she let you?'

'She said it was dangerous. She put a foot on it to test it, then took it off, quickly. The trunk was right across the top of the waterfall, and slippery with moss and wet. She said the wood might be rotten and it might not bear our weight.'

'It sounds to me that Susan acted very sensibly,' I said. 'So you did not use the old tree trunk, but went the proper way, over the footbridge?'

'Yes, sir.'

A moment of silence followed as I digested this snippet of information which, I must admit, I could not link directly to Susan's early morning expedition. It meant I might have to drag some deeper and more relevant piece of information from these girls who clearly thought the incident at the waterfall was of some relevance.

'Ann,' I said. 'Something else happened, didn't it? At the tree trunk over the waterfall? You must tell us – do you think Susan has gone there this morning?'

She nodded and then, quite surprisingly, began to cry. Sylvia McNeil went to her side to comfort her as I pressed ahead with my questioning. I repeated my question,

'Ann, do you think Susan has gone back to the waterfall?'

'She might have, sir.' She rubbed her eyes to brush away the tears.

'Look, Ann, this is important,' I said. 'No one's going to get into trouble, you are not at school now, or at home. You are responsible girls and I want you to act with responsibility. We've got to find Susan in case she's got lost or even hurt herself. Tell me, why do you think Susan might have gone back to the waterfall today?'

'We all said she was scared, sir.'

'Scared? What do you mean?'

Ann licked her lips and looked at Sylvia, then at me. I smiled and asked, 'Who was scared?'

'We all said Susan was scared to cross the trunk, because of the waterfall under it . . . she said she wasn't scared, she said it was dangerous, that's why she wouldn't let us cross it.'

'And was she frightened to cross it?'

'I don't know, sir, she never said. She just said she was our patrol leader and she would not allow us to cross it because it was dangerous. So we didn't. . . .'

'But you argued with her, did you? You said she was scared? Is that it?'

'It was just a bit of fun, sir, we didn't really think she was scared.'

'Ann,' I pressed her, 'if you did not cross the tree trunk because Susan said you shouldn't, why do you think Susan has gone back there now?'

'To cross it, sir. She said she wasn't scared; she said she would cross it herself one day before we finished camp.'

'So you think she's gone there to show herself she can do it?' I asked.

The unhappy girl nodded. 'Yes, sir, I think she might have done that.'

Whether or not that was the real reason for Susan's absence, it did provide a starting point for a search. I knew the waterfall in question – Hagg Foss – for it was about a mile and half upstream from the camp-site in very rocky and hilly surroundings. Hagg Gill tumbled and roared from the higher points of the moor, racing through a narrow, rock-strewn gorge before tumbling over a narrow, lofty ledge into a deep, foam-covered pool below. Once the flow reached the high ledge, it fell directly for about eighty feet in what was locally known as a spout or a foss, churning the pool into which it fell into what looked like a pool of boiling white froth. The two sides of the pool were sheer rock, rich with alpines and rare plants, while the outlet was an open mouth through which the now calm waters flowed. Spectacular though it was, the surrounding rocks and cliffs were full of danger, slippery with water and moss, and deadly if anyone fell from a height.

My next dilemma was whether myself and these Guides (or some of them) were capable of mounting a search and, if we found Susan, dealing with whatever injuries she might have. The area was remote; there was no road anywhere near the waterfall and no communications, my vehicle radio and the telephone kiosk in the village being the only means of contacting the emergency services. The solution was first to find the girl. She might not be hurt; she might be sitting before one of the extensive moorland views in admiration, or watching young foxes at play, or even lying asleep in a shady glade.

If she was not hurt then a full scale call-out of the emergency services or the Ashfordly Search and Rescue Organization seemed superfluous and time-wasting and I began to see that I must first find her and then establish what further assistance was required. I then had a brain-wave, in the use of which every Guide and Guider on this camp could be utilized.

'Sylvia,' I addressed Susan's mother. 'Can we have a quick word? I have an idea, one which might solve our problem of communication.'

'Anything,' she said, the anxiety clear in her eyes.

'I know the path between here and Hagg Foss,' I said. 'It's a good wide footpath, and the distance is about a mile and a half. If we position one Girl Guide every hundred yards or so between my Mini-van and the falls, we could relay a message very quickly indeed. I can leave my Mini-van radio open, connected with Ashfordly Police Station, and all I need do is to shout "Help" if we find Susan needs assistance. I'll decide the precise call when I find out what's happened.'

'But you would actually do the search?'

'Yes, with you and perhaps one other person. And I'd need a responsible adult to make the call on my radio . . . I'd be at the waterfall so I couldn't do it.'

'We've plenty of help,' she assured me. 'And I know the girls would obey all your orders.'

'Right.' With that I went to my Mini-van and called up Ashfordly Police Station. Sergeant Blaketon answered.

'PC Rhea, Sergeant, location – Hagg Carr, Aidensfield, the camp-site. One of the Girl Guides is missing from the camp, Sarge, but I think I know where she is. She might be injured, though. I'm going to leave this radio open, with a responsible adult in attendance, and we're going to search for the lost girl. I have good reason to think she went to Hagg Foss on the moors above the village. I have organized a relay of Girl Guides to get a message to you if I need further assistance, such as a medical team or stretcher-bearers. It will take me about half an hour to get to the waterfall . . . once I'm there, I'll send a message via my relay team and my radio. If she has fallen down the foss, we might need someone with rock-climbing expertise.'

After clarifying a few points, and recording the name of the missing girl, he agreed with my proposals and I next instructed the Guides in establishing the relay I wanted. The adults, group leader and patrol leaders all understood and I left the apportioning of places to them as I set off, walking at brisk pace with Sylvia at my side. Even as I climbed through the trees, I could see the extending line of Girl Guides on the woodland path, each playing her part in the search for Susan McNeil.

It was hot work climbing towards the falls in full uniform, but Sylvia easily kept pace with me. As we approached the falls, their noise guiding us unmistakably towards the scene, we began to call Susan's name, although I feared that if she had fallen anywhere near the foss, the noise of the water would conceal our shouts, just as it would smother her cries for help. But we found her.

She was lying on a high ledge about twenty feet above the pool into which the water fell, having fallen from the tree trunk as she was attempting to prove to herself that she was not afraid. And she had a broken ankle as well as minor abrasions.

She'd been there for almost two hours, shouting to no avail, crying in her terror and distress and was semi-conscious when we arrived. I shouted to rouse her, exhorting her not to attempt to move while adding that help was on the way. Before determining the precise nature of the assistance needed, I managed to clamber to the summit of the wall, using trees and vegetation to haul myself through the rocks, and then managed to look down upon her. Crossing the beck at the point the fall tumbled into the pool below was the long, pale grey remains of a fallen beech tree, some parts covered in moss and others damp and slippery from the moisture it had accumulated. Certainly, it was unsafe as a footbridge.

'Hi, Susan,' I shouted and she waved in response. 'Help's coming. . . .'

I went back to Sylvia and told her Susan was responding but that we needed a stretcher party; I then told her to shout along the relay 'Help, stretcher-party needed, Hagg Foss', followed by

'All Guides to remain at their stations' before coming to the point where she could speak to Susan. And so, as the sound of water roared in my ears, I could hear the first shout, 'Help, stretcher-party needed. . . .'

As I swopped places with Sylvia, herself very nervous in this precarious position, I could hear the shouts growing fainter as the message was passed speedily through the woods, moving at a much faster pace than any runner could have achieved. I just hoped these children would rise to the occasion and not let us down, but they were marvellous. The message reached the Guider who was waiting at my Mini-van, and she called Sergeant Blaketon on my radio.

Instead of calling the ambulance service, Sergeant Blaketon summoned the Ashfordly Search and Rescue Organization because they did have stretcher-bearers with mountaineering and rock-climbing expertise. The short delay in responding to the emergency would be more than compensated by their skills at the scene, and so their van arrived at the camp-site within three-quarters of an hour. They had no trouble finding Susan – they simply followed the line of Girl Guides who had steadfastly remained in position all that time.

To cut short a long story, Susan was rescued and taken to Strensford Hospital for treatment. Although she had a broken right ankle and a few bruises, she was otherwise unhurt, but her friends had been right: Susan had, in fact, been frightened of attempting to cross the log bridge which spanned the top of Hagg Foss and she had declined originally by not admitting she was terrified. Instead, she'd claimed it was dangerous – which it was! On her lone trip to prove herself, she had slipped from it and had crashed down the waterfall, luckily landing on a protruding ledge which had prevented a longer, more dangerous tumble on the rocks in the shallow pool below.

Her mother went to visit her in hospital and, as she stooped to kiss her daughter, Susan said, 'I told them it was dangerous. . . .'

'And your lesson gave them two adventure days!' Her mother gripped her hand tightly. 'But I want no more, not like this one . . . but your friends were great . . . a rescue relay team! How about that?'

'I might join a search and rescue team when I grow up,' said Susan.

'A good idea, so long as you don't attempt to cross any more waterfalls on log bridges!' wept her mother.

5

Better dwell in the midst of alarms
William Cowper (1731–1800)

The North York Moors and the area which surrounds them are each rich with large but extremely remote houses. Some are working farms, some are mansions occupied by the aristocracy, some have been turned into hotels, some are used as shooting lodges, centres for recreation and research or even offices. Sadly, since my time at Aidensfield, several have become deserted and are now little more than sad but atmospheric ruins with the wind sighing through the stones and birds nesting in what remains of their roofs and walls.

Elsinby Grange is one of those large and somewhat mysterious houses but it remains in splendid condition. It is a huge, square edifice built of dark moorland granite with a blue slate roof. For that reason alone it differs from the soft yellow limestone houses of the region, houses which have red pantile roofs often with honeysuckle and roses around the doorways. The imposing front door of Elsinby Grange, fashioned from oak and studded with iron, stands beneath a portico which faces south across a gravelled parking area while the huge front windows of the reception-room, morning-room and dining-room gaze across an uninterrupted view of the moors. One corner of the house comprises a rounded turret structure while a blue-faced clock is prominent upon another tower behind the main house. Also behind the house is a conglomeration of outbuildings large and small, a legacy of the days when this was the home farm of a massive estate.

During the estate's days of glory, the main house was Elsinby Hall, the home of the Marquis of Elsinby, but soon after the estate was broken up and sold to pay the death duties of the last marquis, the Hall caught fire and was totally destroyed. The sole surviving house in what had been the grounds of the former Elsinby Hall was Home Farm. This, along with some forty acres which surrounded it, was purchased by a London property developer, drastically modernized and renamed Elsinby Grange. That is the name by which I have always known the house.

It stood – and still stands – on a lofty finger of land high above the village of Elsinby. It is the only house on that elevated site, the remainder of the finger comprising copses, scrubland, grassland and the extensive gardens of the house. The lower slopes of the finger are covered with a dense mixture of coniferous and deciduous trees which serve to conceal the house from below; quite literally, it is impossible, even during the winter months, to see the house from any vantage point in the village or the neighbouring dale. Even when walking on the surrounding hills, Elsinby Grange is practically invisible, in spite of its size and position, the only way to gain a proper view being from the air. Indeed, helicopters did occasionally fly into the grounds of the Grange for they were spacious enough to admit them.

Road access, however, was via a steeply ascending and winding track which snaked through the trees from an ever-closed gate. That gate was at the end of a cul-de-sac and next to the churchyard in Elsinby; at first glance, a visitor might think the gate led only into the church grounds, but it followed the line of the eastern boundary wall of the churchyard before veering up the hill and through the trees.

Even from that gate, it was impossible to see the house on the top of the hill. The local people knew about the almost secret entrance to the Grange and in their mind it was not unusual, but few casual visitors ever guessed there was such a splendid building on the hill behind the façade of trees. This illusion was furthered by the fact that the name of Elsinby Grange did not feature on the gate or anywhere near it. Thus, there was nothing in Elsinby to suggest the presence of the house and I know that visiting delivery men had trouble finding the place.

Indeed, it was some time before I knew the house was there. Although Elsinby was a village for which I was responsible as a village policeman, there was never any reason to visit the Grange. It was not a working farm; consequently, I did not have to inspect the owner's stock registers or firearms certificates, neither did I have to visit the house for any other purpose. It was virtually a secret house.

Inevitably, there was an air of mystery about it. Its occupants often came under cover of darkness and there were times we knew the house was occupied only because there was an occasional glimpse of lights behind the trees or a stranger calling at the shop for provisions. The owners of the Grange did not employ local people to clean or maintain the premises or its grounds, consequently no one in Elsinby really knew who was coming and going. Some of the people who came for holidays or weekends brought their own staff; it was they who did the shopping. At times the gardens and grounds would be cared for by teams of visiting specialists. After a while, I realized the house was a haven or retreat for the rich and famous, people who wanted to get away from public gaze if only for a few days.

This dawned on me when I carried out a routine check of a motor car which I'd seen prowling around Elsinby at two o'clock one Saturday morning. After cruising slowly through the village several times, it vanished along Church Lane just as I managed to obtain its registration number, and then made for Elsinby Grange. I saw the lights climbing the hill – and later, when I received the result of my enquiries, I discovered the car was owned by Jason Ridgeway, a well-known and very popular television personality of the time. It was that discovery that prompted me to make a few discreet enquiries and I was able to establish that that was the new function of Elsinby Grange. It was let to famous people who wanted a bit of peace and quiet and it was soon clear to me that the establishment was run in an amazingly secretive manner. Quite literally, we never knew who was in residence there.

Several people in the village knew the secret of the Grange but, right from the beginning of the enterprise, they had been asked to exercise discretion, particularly if members of the public and adoring fans came seeking their heroes and heroines. The usual places of enquiry by tourists and fans were the post office, pub and village shop, but the proprietors of those establishments always shook their heads and denied any knowledge of the presence of famous people in the village and said there was no such hiding place in tiny Elsinby. In that way, the people of Elsinby helped to protect the famous people who came to relax among them – and that served only to encourage more famous people to visit this tiny place. From time to time, I became privy to secret visits by some of the world's most famous people, but I never revealed my knowledge to anyone.

On the other hand, famous people came and went without me, or anyone else in the district, knowing of their presence. Although most of the Grange visitors never emerged during their stay, there was one occasion when Bing Crosby called at the Hopbind Inn for a drink, minus his toupee. The pub was full of tourists at the time and no one recognized him. Charlie Chaplin was another visitor to the Grange, as were some of the Beatles, various film and television stars, singers, actors and musicians. Prominent politicians came too, both from Britain and the United States, and on more than one occasion, various members of the British Royal Family have stayed quietly at Elsinby Grange.

Not once did I have any worries or problems, but then a disturbing rumour began to circulate one September. It reached my ears fairly early in its infancy – and it was to the effect that some of the Great Train Robbers, i.e. those who had not been quickly arrested, were in hiding at Elsinby Grange. I bore in mind that this particular rumour had been heard in most of the villages of England, especially those with large and remote houses, but it was a tale that I could not ignore.

That famous robbery occurred in the early hours of Thursday,

8 August, 1963 when the Royal Mail train from Glasgow to Euston was stopped by a team of armed robbers at Sears Crossing near Linslade which was then in Buckinghamshire. The raiders were armed and something like £2.5 million was stolen, then the largest amount of cash known to have been the subject of such a raid. Thanks to the fairly swift discovery of the robbers' hideout some twenty miles away at premises known as Leatherslade Farm, several of the perpetrators were arrested. Furthermore, a small amount of stolen money was also recovered, all these events being prior to my arrival at Aidensfield. Even with the passage of a few years, the robbery remained in the public consciousness due partly to the audacity of the raiders, but also because some of the participants, whose names were known to the police, were still being hunted – along with more than £2 million of stolen cash.

People throughout Britain were fascinated by this crime even though the unfortunate train driver, Jack Mills, later died following injuries he received during the raid. In the years immediately following the robbery, there were many reported rumours and claimed sightings of alleged train robbers in hiding, in some cases proving to be innocent people seeking peace and solitude whereas in others the suspected birds had flown – so the police never knew whether or not they'd just missed the fleeing robbers.

But now I had such a rumour on my own quiet rural patch. In view of the secrecy which always surrounded the people in residence at Elsinby Grange, I knew that such a thing was not impossible and it might even be feasible for the raiders to gain legal access to the house through the help of friends in so-called high places. With the right amount of money and the backing of agents and helpers, almost anything is possible and in the case of Elsinby Grange, its ability to maintain secrecy for its clients had been proved many times. There were many reasons for persons in hiding to come to such a place. As a police officer, however, I knew the dangers of attaching too much credence to a mere rumour and it was important that I established whether or not there was any truth in this one.

If there was any truth whatsoever, then action would have to be taken, probably in the form of a raid on the premises by highly trained police officers and so, without losing any time, I began to investigate the source of this tale. My first problem was that I must approach this with care – if I started to ask questions in the village, it would serve only to give credibility to the rumour – and my second problem was that no one could tell me where or how the yarn had started.

My first approach was George, the landlord of the local pub. The Hopbind Inn was always a port of call for me during my patrols, although it was not my practice to drink alcohol while on duty. My visits were purely for police purposes and on this occasion I arrived during the lunchtime opening hours. The place was busy with local drinkers including Claude Jeremiah Greengrass. I was pleased he was there – I knew that if a rumour was circulating, he would know about it. My job was to tempt him to repeat it and perhaps to expand upon it, albeit with just a little bait – getting Claude to air his knowledge or to claim the police were not doing their job would not be difficult. On this occasion, Claude was my unwitting start to this low-key start to my investigation.

'How's things in Elsinby, George?' was my opening gambit as I watched him pull a frothy pint for a customer.

'Same as usual, Nick,' he said. 'Quiet, no bother.'

'The holiday season's over.' I tried to make light conversation. 'I suppose that reduces your casual custom – but you've got these regulars to keep you busy. And I don't think we've anybody in the Grange this week.'

At that comment, Greengrass piped up, 'If that's what you think, Constable, you're not doing your job. Train robbers. That's who's in the Grange. Hiding there, holed up so nobody can see 'em. Them who's not been caught.'

'That's rumour, Claude, nothing but rumour.' I tried to make light of this while at the same time attempting to glean any useful information. 'They've been seen in every holiday cottage and rural pub in England over the past year or so. In fact, I don't think there's a cottage anywhere that's not had one or other of the train robbers there in hiding, that's if we believe all the stories.'

'Aye, well, they've got to be somewhere and there's no smoke without fire, that's what I say. You want to get yourself up there and knock on the door, and take Blaketon, Ventress and the rest of your mates with you because the spot is full of train robbers and their minders. That's what I've heard.'

'You've been conned, Claude,' I added more bait now. 'It's folks pulling your leg. Besides, it would take more than Blaketon, Ventress and me to surround the place and execute a successful raid.'

'You're dead right! There's some heavies up there, Constable, make no mistake about it. Watching the doors and patrolling the grounds; nobody'll ever get near the place. And they don't come down here for their bits of shopping . . . they never leave the place. Came by night, they did, last Saturday. . . .'

'You've been up there, have you?' I put to him.

'Me? Not likely, mate! You'll not catch me risking my neck in them woods when those chaps are about.'

'Has anybody else heard this rumour?' I directed my question at George, but I knew it would be heard by all the men in the bar.

'I heard it, Mr Rhea,' said a quietly spoken farmer. 'Third- or fourth-hand mind, but somebody told my mate the train robbers were hiding there. The chap who told him sometimes supplies milk when folks are in the Grange. He was pretty certain about it because he's been ordered to leave a crate at the bottom gate, that's the one in Church Lane, every day this week. Twelve pints. A lot of milk, Mr Rhea, so there's obviously a few folks living there. Twelve pints a day takes a bit of supping. But he was told he had no need to take it right up to the house. He reckons they don't want him to see who's staying there.'

'So who's likely to know the names of these people who arrange the rental of the Grange?' I asked George.

'No idea,' he admitted. 'I've never known, Nick. It's all done from offices in London. I haven't their address or phone number, they're not keen for such things to become common knowledge. It's not often we get to know who's in residence, then we can't let the Press know. To be honest, I don't want to know who's renting the place then I can't be criticized for gossiping about them. But this tale about the train robbers has been pretty strong, I must admit.'

'What did I tell you?' smirked Claude. 'You're not seeing the obvious, Constable. Just imagine – a wanted man or mebbe more than one living on your patch and you know nowt about it! You and your mates shut your eyes to real criminals and persecute innocent blokes like me who're struggling to earn a decent living.'

As I chatted to the customers in the pub, it appeared that the rumour had some foundation although I knew enough about the characters involved to realize a lot of it would be due to imagination and speculation fuelled by fancy rather than hard fact. Nonetheless, I decided I must establish just who was currently living at the Grange; but I felt I had to do so very discreetly – if it was the men or even just one man currently being sought for the Great Train Robbery, I did not want to frighten him or them away. I wanted any villain to be arrested – and it would be nice to have them caught on my own small patch of England. Upon leaving the Hopbind Inn, therefore, I went for a chat with Gilbert Kingston who ran the local post office and delivered the village mail.

'I've not had any mail for the Grange,' he told me, as I tried to establish whether any names had been referred to. 'It's not often I get stuff for the temporary residents, although circulars sometimes arrive. More often than not, if the residents are expecting anything by post, they send a minion down to pick it up.'

'So who's living there now?' I asked him.

'Search me.' He shrugged his shoulders. 'I've never been near the place. I did hear they arrived late one night or in the early hours of the morning and some daft bat has spread a tale that it's some of the Great Train Robbers.'

'You don't believe that?' I smiled.

'No way!' he said. 'The folks they get into that place are the cream; politicians, royals, moneyed folks, not criminals and their like.'

'Not even criminals with a few million quid to spend?' I put to him.

'I would think whoever comes to stay there gets vetted pretty closely by the owners before any agreement is made,' he said. 'It's a very posh place, Nick, like a top-class hotel in many ways or a very posh holiday home; hardly the spot to find criminals on the run. You'd sooner find Princess Margaret or Cliff Richard in the house.'

'So I can dismiss the rumours?' I said.

'Well, it's up to you, Nick, I can't tell you how to do your job, but it would surprise me if we got villains living there, even for a weekend and even if they are stinking rich, legally or otherwise.'

Thus I had two conflicting and very local views and; as I patrolled the village trying to sift truth from rumour, I had words with several Elsinby stalwarts, including Harold Poulter, the undertaker, Dr Archie McGee, Samuel Cook, the cobbler, and Father Brendan O'Malley, the parish priest at the Catholic Church of St Francis of Assisi. All had heard the rumours but all dismissed them as being typical of the rumours that sometimes circulated in rural areas. But when I went into the village shop, now owned and run by a couple who'd left Birmingham for a quiet rural life, I got a different story. These were John and Betty Belshaw. Elsinby shop was a tiny place which occupied the front room of a cottage which overlooked the stream. It would hardly support a single person but John and Betty had each retired from lucrative posts in industry and had useful pensions. They ran the shop more as a social service than a profit-making enterprise but did manage to cover costs. I do know their efforts were appreciated.

John, a small balding man in his late sixties, was behind the tiny counter when I entered.

'Good afternoon, Nick,' he smiled. 'It's not often we see you in here.'

'It's business, John,' I told him. 'I'm trying to establish who we've got in the Grange just now.'

'You've heard the story then? About some of the Great Train Robbers being there? Isn't it exciting . . . are you going to raid the place?'

'I need to find out for certain before I decide what action to take, that's why I'm asking around. At the moment, it just seems like a silly rumour.'

'Well,' he said, lowering his voice as if we were being overheard, 'one of my delivery men said he'd been asked to drop stuff at the house and to keep his mouth shut . . . he came here and reckoned it was that Wilson chap, the one who escaped from Winsom Green Prison. That's not far from where we come from, you know, it's on Winsom Green Road in Birmingham.'

'Charles Frederick Wilson!' I spoke the name because I recalled it from the posters and circulars we had received.

'He got thirty years for armed robbery and twenty-five years on another charge, then he escaped from prison. He's not been seen since,' whispered John. 'My mate reckons it's him. He's got a few minders, they won't let you anywhere near the house.'

'Did your pal actually see Wilson?' I asked.

'No,' he said. 'No, he couldn't get anywhere near the house, the minders came out and dealt with the delivery, then he was asked to leave, but he heard one of them whisper something about Wilson. They saw him off the premises. That was yesterday.'

'Well, thanks. So what I must do now is to establish whether there is reasonable grounds for suspecting that a prison escapee is hiding there. . . .'

'There's no doubt in my mind, Nick, and you've been pretty quick establishing that . . . so the next thing will be a raid, you think? Armed police coming to Elsinby with Black Marias and police dogs. . . .'

'More like me and Sergeant Blaketon going to the front door to ask if Charles Frederick Wilson is in!' I laughed.

'You'd never get near the place, they'd see you coming and be out of the back door like a flash . . . you'll need lots of police to surround the place and keep the helicopters from landing and so on. . . .'

I could see that this little shopkeeper had a fairly vivid imagination, but in some aspects, he was right. Blaketon, Ventress, myself and the constables of Ashfordly were hardly capable of surrounding Elsinby Grange to carry out a sophisticated raid on the well-protected hideout of a Great Train Robber, and so I had to seek the opinions of higher authority. I radioed Ashfordly Police Station to see if Sergeant Blaketon was on duty. He was, and answered my call.

Rather than risk being overheard on air, I told Blaketon I had received some important information and suggested a rendezvous.

He said he would come immediately and I proposed a meeting at Ploatby, a short distance from Elsinby. Our presence would not, therefore, fuel the rumours or alarm the occupants of the Grange. Sergeant Blaketon arrived in Ploatby some fifteen minutes later and I joined him in his official car.

'So, Rhea, what's all the mystery?' he asked, his face showing some evident excitement.

'There are rumours that the Great Train Robber, the one who escaped from prison . . .'

'Wilson,' he said, his eyes bright with anticipation. He'd read the circulars too.

'Yes, Charles Frederick Wilson. Well, Sergeant, the rumours say he's holed up at Elsinby Grange with a band of minders.' I followed this with a description of the house and how it was widely used as a discreet holiday home. I explained about the rumours and how I had tried to determine whether or not there was any truth in them, giving him details of the stealthy arrival of the occupants and how their supplies had to be left at the gate near the church, a long distance from the house. And how the tradesman had heard a whispered reference to Wilson.

He listened carefully, pursing his lips from time to time and when I had finished, he said, 'You realize, Rhea, that Wilson and his mates have been reported seen or living in every town, village and country pub in Great Britain. . . .'

'Yes, I know that, Sergeant. But in our case I felt this rumour had to be examined with great care.'

'So what are you suggesting, Rhea?' he put to me.

'Well, I think we need to visit the house, Sergeant, and even search it.'

'And scare them off? They'll see us coming a mile off. This one's too big for us, Rhea, if it's true, that is. I think I must have words with higher authority, like Inspector Breckon at Eltering. I'll call him now.'

'Over the air?' I asked. 'If these are the robbers, they'll be listening in to our broadcasts. They'll be off like a shot if they know we're on to them.'

'Good thinking!' he said. 'Right, let's go to your police house and ring from there.'

In a small procession, we drove our own vehicles to the Aidensfield police house where I showed him into my office and asked Mary to produce a pot of tea. As he sat at my desk, I stood beside the counter, awaiting the official reaction to this dramatic development.

'It's Blaketon, sir, speaking from Aidensfield police house,' Blaketon introduced himself. 'Rhea has been investigating a rumour that one or more of the Great Train Robbers are holed up in a house on his patch. Elsinby Grange, sir, it's used as an expensive holiday home by pop stars and the like. All very remote and secret,' and he followed this with an outline of what I had told him and why I believed the rumour to have substance.

I could not hear the inspector's responses, but after a moment, Blaketon said, 'Names? Well, sir, his local intelligence suggests it could be Wilson, sir. Charles Frederick Wilson.'

After another pause, Blaketon said, 'Well, sir, we'd need back-up with more officers and dogs, and a search warrant, and even firearms . . . it's a very difficult place to approach unseen, sir. . . .'

There was another pause and then Blaketon said, 'Very good, sir,' and replaced the telephone.

'He's ringing the superintendent,' he told me. 'He'll call us back here, so we must wait.'

And so we enjoyed Mary's cups of tea as we chatted about the Great Train Robbery which continued to captivate police officers and civilians alike. Blaketon grew quite excited about the possibility of his officers actually capturing such a notorious escapee, and then the phone rang. I answered it.

'Superintendent here, Rhea,' he said. 'Is your sergeant there?'

'Yes, sir, I'll put him on,' and I passed the handset to Sergeant Blaketon.

I could not hear what the superintendent was saying but soon Sergeant Blaketon's face grew very red and embarrassed and eventually he replaced the phone, tight-lipped and angry.

'It *is* Wilson, Rhea,' he said shortly. 'The man in your secret hideway is Wilson. Harold Wilson, the prime minster. He's staying at Elsinby Grange and no one, other than a chosen few, is supposed to know. Even we are not supposed to know. *You* are not supposed to know. The superintendent wants a report from you and me, explaining how you knew he was there when it is such a closely guarded secret. Heads will roll, Rhea, heads will roll!'

'Yes, Sergeant,' I replied, somewhat relieved that we hadn't raided the place with dozens of policemen, guns and dogs. That was not the sort of action by the police that would have pleased a Labour Government.

A much smaller house provided another mystery for me in Aidensfield. It was one of those tiny village cottages that people tended to overlook because it was hidden behind others and access was by a narrow footpath between two larger properties on the main street. It was impossible to gain access with a motor vehicle, except perhaps a small motor bike, because the footpath itself was only one-person wide and quite overgrown with weeds. Some fifty yards along it, however, stood Jasmine Cottage with its yellow door, blue woodwork around the windows, red tiles and green wooden railings. On the few occasions I had to visit the house, I thought it looked like something out of *Snow White and the Seven Dwarfs*, or a house from some other part of Disney's wonderful world.

The owner/occupier was Miss Gallant. Everyone knew her by that name and her house was sometimes referred to as Miss Gallant's Cottage because she had lived there for as long as anyone could remember. I never found any living person who could recall the house without Miss Gallant. She was a short but sturdy woman of indeterminate age with a head of iron-grey hair always held in place on top of her head with a red ribbon and a huge bow. The possessor of a very loud voice and cultured accent, she dressed in long, flowing, very colourful clothes which were almost theatrical. This distinctive appearance was enhanced by her highly polished, black, lace-up boots of the kind Victorian ladies used to wear and the purple parasol she always carried whatever the weather.

I reckoned she was well into her eighties when I was policing Aidensfield and during the course of my work, I learned she had no family. There were no brothers and sisters, nieces or nephews and although she did have a wide circle of friends in the district who popped in to visit her, no members of her family ever called. For that reason, everyone assumed, quite naturally, that she was a spinster without any relations.

Miss Gallant was one of the village characters. She was always called Miss Gallant because no one knew her Christian name and even her friends referred to her in that rather old-fashioned formal manner. Nonetheless, she was universally liked; she appeared to be financially sound and she could often be seen pottering up to the shop or the post office for her daily provisions where she placed her orders in her booming, commanding voice. I discovered that, in her younger days, she was often away from Aidensfield, sometimes travelling overseas and sometimes leaving her cottage for two or three weeks at a stretch, or even for just a weekend. For that reason, she never kept pets or livestock, and was content to live in such a tiny home. Because she had no car, she travelled by train, but always walked to her village destinations or took Arnold Merryweather's bus if she had to visit her bank in Ashfordly. In recent years, probably due to her age, her travels had been much reduced and now Aidensfield was the focus of her life.

She would always make an appearance at village events and was a firm supporter of the village hall, being a long-serving member of its committee. She voiced a strong belief that the hall should be the focal point for activities in the community, not the pub. Another of her keen interests was the Anglican church choir where she was a prominent soloist if the occasion demanded. Her strong, fine contralto voice was beautiful. Even in her advancing age she could fill our village hall with the sound of her singing whenever she was called to take part in a pantomime or concert of any kind. She never needed a microphone either and I reckon she could have out-shouted any sergeant-major had a contest ever been arranged.

Then one Friday lunchtime, Maisie Shepherd, the Aidensfield post woman, called at my house. A widow in her late fifties, Maisie delivered the mail in the village and at isolated farms and houses around the outskirts. She used her official red pedal cycle which had a huge iron-framed letter and parcel tray on the front; at Christmas, this was piled so high with parcels that she had to push the cycle because she couldn't see over the top. A large, no-nonsense lady, she was the ears and eyes of Aidensfield, her work taking her quite literally to every home in the village, and during her tours she made sure she checked the most vulnerable members of our community. She called them 'my old folks' although some were younger than she; she would light their fires, collect their shopping or pensions, sit and chat for a while and even do the washing-up – and she did all this even if it led to delays in the delivery of the mail.

Although she displayed a very brusque manner, she was a kindly lady whose unofficial help was always appreciated, and the discovery of those in need was one of her strengths – even if some thought she was a nosy-parker.

On this occasion, I was on duty and enjoying my meal break at the time but when I opened the door, I knew from the expression of Maisie's face that she had encountered something unpleasant.

'It's Miss Gallant,' she said softly. 'I went to her cottage, Nick, to check she's all right like I do most Fridays, but it's all locked up. There's a bottle of milk on the doorstep and her *Daily Telegraph* is still in the letter-box. I shouted and knocked, but got no reply. The front-room curtains are closed, by the way; she always closes them at night. She was all right yesterday, and said nothing about going away. She always lets me know, if she's not going to be at home.'

'I'll go straight away,' I assured her. 'Can you come with me? I might need help.'

'Yes, of course.'

Five minutes later, we arrived at Miss Gallant's cottage and found it as Maisie had said. We toured the front and back to ensure there was no sign of a break-in, then I knocked on the front and rear doors, shouting her name at the same time. There was no response, the place was utterly quiet. As Maisie had told me, the downstairs curtains were closed but I noticed her bedroom curtains were open which suggested she had not gone to bed last night. After several bouts of shouting and knocking, I decided I had to gain entry to the cottage.

If at all possible, I did not want to smash a window or force open one of the doors – that was guaranteed to cause problems in the future if only to determine who should effect any repairs – so I toured the house and eventually found a rear bedroom window which was slightly open. I borrowed a ladder from a neighbouring garden shed, climbed up, opened the window to its full extent and clambered in. Maisie waited below. As I crawled into the house, I shouted to her that I would open the front door if the key was in the lock.

I found myself in a small back bedroom which smelt of mothballs and which looked like something from a Victorian film set with a tiny cast-iron fireplace and a brass bedstead, but I had no time to admire the antique furnishings as I hurried through. I raced down the well-carpeted stairs, unlocked the front door with the key which, fortunately, was in the lock, and admitted Maisie. I took the milk and *Daily Telegraph* into the house. Then, as Maisie stood in the hall, I entered the front room, the one with the drawn curtains. In the gloom, I could see a rocking chair before the dead coal-fire, a pair of feet protruding from it – small feet, a lady's feet, clad in black leather boots.

'Miss Gallant,' I called, gently at first as I tapped on the door. But there was no response. I wondered if she had fallen asleep in her rocking chair, so I shouted again, much louder this time, and rapped harder on the door. But there was no response.

Maisie had followed me into the room and I asked her to open the heavy green velvet curtains.

As she did so, the room was bathed in daylight which was cast upon the still form in the chair. Miss Gallant did not stir among all this activity. I approached her gently, calling her name, all the time sensing she was long past caring. With no response from her, I reached out and touched her cheek – it was cold. She was dead. I knew from her apprearance that she had been dead for some hours and my initial belief was that she had died sometime last night while sitting in front of her fire. There was a book on the floor beside her. I reasoned it had tumbled from her grasp as she had slipped into oblivion.

'She's gone,' I said to Maisie. 'There's nothing we can do for her now.' I returned to the window to close the curtains.

'Poor old thing,' she said. 'She was such a lovely, interesting old lady, but at least she's died peacefully. I think that's how she would want to go, Nick; it's a lovely way really.'

'There's no sign of pain on her face,' I added. 'She's totally at peace.'

'So what happens now?' asked Maisie.

'I have to examine her very briefly to make sure she has not been attacked, and I must then examine the interior of the house to make sure there's been no illegal entry or crime against her or her home. If there are no suspicious circumstances, I can treat it as a routine sudden death. In any case, I've got to call in Doctor Williams to certify she's dead and if he can't certify the cause of her death, it'll mean a post-mortem examination, so the coroner will have to be informed. And I have to find her relatives to get her formally identified.'

'I don't think she has any,' Maisie said. 'I've never known any of them visit her or write to her.'

'She must have somebody,' I countered. 'It might mean a search of her letters and family papers . . . not a very pleasant job, but if we can't get her formally identified, it'll have to be done. But first, I must examine her.'

My examination was, of necessity, very brief – it entailed a look at her face, head, neck, hands and other exposed places for any sign of a wound, then, easing her forward in the chair to ensure there were no wounds in her back or spinal area or the back of her head, and checking for signs of blood about her clothing. I found none. There were no empty bottles of pills or medicines beside her and I was sure that Miss Gallant had not been attacked, nor had she taken her own life. A tour of the interior of the house, with Maisie in attendance, likewise assured me that no one had unlawfully entered Jasmine Cottage – there was no sign of a housebreaking, theft or attempted crime of any sort such as arson or malicious damage. Maisie was familiar with the contents and state of the cottage, being a regular visitor to Miss Gallant and she supported my assessment.

'I can safely say this is not a suspicious death,' I said to Maisie. 'But thanks for being with me. Now, I must lock up the house and call the doctor.'

Doctor Williams was, by chance, visiting patients in Aidensfield and I was able to locate him very quickly and escort him into Jasmine Cottage. He certified the death of Miss Gallant, but said he could not certify the cause of her death because he had not attended her for some five years.

This meant the coroner had to be notified and so I rang his office. After listening to my account, he ordered a post-mortem; I arranged for her body to be removed to the mortuary of Strensford Hospital for the post-mortem to be conducted as soon as possible. Next I'd have to find someone who could make a formal identification of the body. Ideally, that should be a relative. The problem was that most people in the village, including myself and Maisie, knew her as Miss Gallant – and that was all. So far as I was aware, none knew her Christian name. I could truthfully state that this was the body of the woman I knew as Miss Gallant, but was that her real name and did I really know her? I had no knowledge of her past, no idea of her date of birth, her full name, her home district, her former work or anything else, and I knew I had to return to the house to search it for her personal papers. The coroner would require me to ensure that she was formally identified before authorizing the burial.

After Maurice Merryman, the undertaker, had removed the body to the mortuary, I remained in the house to search for evidence of positive identification. Although I did not conduct a meticulous search of every piece of paper or storage place, I found her bureau. It was full of personal things including writing paper, envelopes, several fountain pens and bottles of different coloured inks but there was no birth certificate, marriage certificate, passport, will or other document of identification. Surprisingly, there were no unanswered letters, although I did find a small file of her rate demands and electricity bills, all paid through the very exclusive Blackstone's Bank.

It had a branch in Ashfordly, Ashfordly being the central market town for an area rich with members of the aristocracy and landed gentry. It was widely known that they made use of this bank. It made me wonder why Miss Gallant made use of Blackstone's instead of one of the well-known high street banks because she had never struck me as being a member of the nobility, or an upper-class person or even being suitably wealthy.

During my search of the house, however, I had no trouble locating her pension book and some cash in a money box. From the pension book, I learned that her first name was Letitia and the pension book contained her National Insurance number which might help if I needed to make further enquiries. I removed the cash and counted it – there was nearly £200, a lot of money to have in the house and so I removed it, placed a receipt in the box and took the cash for onward transmission to Ashfordly Police Station for safe-keeping. I was now aware that the little house was a possible target for those sharks who prey on the homes of the deceased, sometimes with removal vans –

but in this case, they'd have difficulty transporting the heavy furniture along the narrow path. Someone must have had to exercise great skill in getting the larger items into the house – but the prospect of ready cash is always a temptation to unscrupulous villains.

I took possession of her formal documents – the pension book, rate demands, electricity bills and so forth, because they would provide some evidence of her identity and then I left the house. I took the unopened bottle of milk with me; I would give it to old Mr Fishpool at the council houses. He was a gentleman whom I knew was desperately short of money and whom, I knew, was often given food by Miss Gallant. Allowing him to have the milk was the sort of thing Miss Gallant would have done herself. Then I locked the door. As I walked away from the tiny cottage, I turned to look back – it was such a charming place, so unusual and in many ways utterly unique – and it then dawned upon me that I had not seen a solitary family photograph in any of the rooms.

It was extremely rare, I felt, for someone not to have at least one family portrait or picture in the house and with that thought, I walked away. As I left the house, I wondered if this was the prelude to an interesting enquiry during which I must positively identify the lady that everyone knew as Miss Gallant. From the office at my police house, I rang Sergeant Blaketon to notify him of the sudden death and outlined the work I had undertaken, finally explaining that I had arranged a post-mortem at Strensford Hospital.

He expressed satisfaction and asked, 'Have you informed the relatives?'

'She hasn't any, Sergeant,' I told him.

'She must have somebody! Who's going to make the formal identification? You'll need that for the Registrar of Births, Deaths and Marriages, won't you? Where's her birth certificate, Rhea?'

I told him I had been unable to locate it, although I had her pension book, rate demands and so forth, all bearing the name we knew.

'They're no good for *positive* proof, Rhea! Evidence, yes; proof, no. Anybody could have got hold of those! So who is this old dear? I think it's very strange no one has ever used her Christian name, she has no family pictures about the place and there's no sign of anything else to positively prove who she is. Proof, Rhea, you need proof, not bits of paper and books with just a name on. Get back to the house and give it a thorough search. We don't want to have a person buried in somebody else's name, do we? And it's the relatives' job to arrange the funeral, so you must trace someone with responsibility for her. We can't leave her lying about unburied!'

I thought he was perhaps being rather too cautious for I could not imagine Miss Gallant being the sort of lady to steal someone else's pension book and adopt that person's name . . . but you could never be sure. A further search of the house was called for, however distressing that might be. Wondering where to begin, I let myself in and began at her bureau. As with my earlier search, I failed to locate any of her official documents such as the birth certificate or her will and after removing every scrap of paper, piece by piece, I was convinced those documents were not in the bureau which she appeared to have used as her desk. This meant I had to literally examine every drawer, cupboard, loft, box and other possible hiding place. Old people were notorious for hiding important things in places even they forgot – I knew one old lady who, one summer, concealed a large amount of cash in the ashes bin of her fireplace. Then, in winter, she forgot about the money, lit the fire and the falling ashes burnt several hundred pounds' worth of bank notes.

Another hid her money in a flour bag, the notes not mixing very well when she tried to bake a cake, while an old man hid his cash in the pocket of an old jacket which he gave to a passing tramp – complete with a pocketful of five pound notes. The tramp and his windfall of £500 were never found.

It was with these thoughts in mind that I started a very detailed search of the house, beginning with Miss Gallant's bedroom. The bedroom was furnished with beautiful antiques and I felt very much a trespasser as I undertook my distasteful duty, but, by a stroke of good fortune, I found what I wanted in a small drawer of her dressing-table. In a white envelope, I found a key labelled 'Safe Deposit Box, Blackstone's Bank, Ashfordly'. I took possession of it and then made a search of the other drawers and the wardrobe without finding any papers. But I felt sure the key would provide me with a starting point and decided to visit the bank before searching any further. Half an hour later, I was in the office of John Barlow, the youthful and smartly dressed manager of Blackstone's Bank in Ashfordly.

In detail, I explained what had happened to Miss Gallant and how my search had not revealed any family members; I also stressed I had to ensure she was positively identified before the coroner would authorize her burial and then I produced the safe deposit box key. I asked if, in these rather exceptional circumstances, I could be allowed to examine her box with a view to establishing her identity and, if possible, tracing family members. I told him that I was in need of two things – her birth certificate if it was available, or perhaps a passport bearing a photograph, and her will she had made one. That might contain her funeral wishes.

'Every case must be dealt with on its merits,' Mr Barlow explained. 'Now, before we go any further, let me examine our register to see precisely what we are keeping for her.'

Having checked in a register, he told me she had in safe keeping with the bank, one large brown envelope sealed by her, the contents of which were unknown to the bank staff, and a safe deposit box, the key of which I now possessed. Whereas it was normal in some circumstances for a court order to be necessary for someone other than the owner to examine such deposit boxes, in these circumstances, I could look into the envelope, albeit in the presence of two members of the bank staff. However, I could not remove anything from the bank and a note would be placed inside the envelope to record what had transpired this day.

Mr Barlow called for his deputy to join us and to bring in Miss Gallant's brown envelope and her safe deposit box. As

Barlow arranged a cup of coffee for us all, the articles arrived courtesy of Alan Scott, his deputy. The large brown envelope was sealed with some wax and initialled by Miss Gallant with her name beneath the initials. Taking care not to tear it, John Barlow opened the envelope and extracted the contents which he spread across his desk. Among them was a birth certificate and an expired passport. I picked up the passport – it contained her photograph, now well out of date, and her name. John Barlow said he could confirm that the lady who was his customer was the lady in that photograph, i.e. Letitia Gallant, and he would be happy to swear to that fact before the coroner. I took down in my notebook details of the passport, such as its date and place of issue.

Then I opened the birth certificate. As I had now come to expect, it recorded the birth of Letitia Gallant on 4 September 1872, but then I saw that her father was shown as Vernon Gallant, otherwise Viscount Galtreford, a landowner, and her mother was Diana Josephine Gallant, Viscountess Galtreford. Inside the envelope was a note saying her will was in the safe deposit box, along with instructions for her funeral. That provided us with the authority to open the safe deposit box. It contained some jewellery and small items of silver, but there was a will tied in red ribbon, and a note saying 'my funeral arrangements'.

Everything was very simple. She wanted to be buried in Aidensfield Anglican parish church yard, the costs to be met from the sale of her house, its contents and her jewellery. Her solicitors would make the necessary arrangements. She did not want the Galtreford family to be involved because they had rejected her when she had decided upon a career on the stage and so she never used the title 'Honourable'. From the sale of her estate, she nominated a number of beneficiaries, including several local charities, albeit with a substantial sum (£15,000) going to Aidensfield village hall for whatever purposes the management committee decided.

Thus I could confirm her identity and we now knew her wishes – and we had someone, her solicitor, to make all the necessary arrangements. I felt this was a rather sad end to a remarkable old lady, but her heart had been in Aidensfield and now her mortal remains would lie there for eternity. I thanked the two bankers and went to inform her solicitors, Simpson, Hurley and Briggs of Ashfordly.

It was some weeks later, when the funeral was over and while the house was being cleared, that the removal men found a large box of yellowed newspaper cuttings featuring the famous music-hall singer and comedienne, Letty Noble. That's who she was. The Honourable Letitia Gallant had been Letty Noble, famous in her day as a singer, entertainer and comedienne in the music halls of this country, but her aristocratic upbringing had always caused her to be formally addressed as Miss Gallant. One did not use Christian names when addressing that class of person, there were formalities to be respected.

For all that, she was a lovely lady who now lies in Aidensfield church yard where her gravestone bears the name Letitia Gallant. Her contribution to the village hall funds is marked by a plaque inside the building and the Letitia Gallant Cup is given every year to the most promising singer in the village, male or female. Neither her aristocratic ancestry nor her music-hall fame are recorded in the churchyard or in the village hall and her little house is now a holiday cottage which is popular with tourists.

6

Hail, glorious edifice, stupendous work!
James Smith (1775–1839) and
Horace Smith (1779–1849)

For as long as humans have inhabited the North York Moors, they have erected upon those heathery heights, a quite astonishing range of structures, some useful, some decorative and some with an unknown purpose. These vary from the ultra-modern Ballistic Missile Early Warning Station on Fylingdales Moor by way of grouse butts and follies to simple standing stones with ancient or prehistoric significance. To these we can add the giant landmark which is the White Horse of Kilburn, Austin Wright's abstract and thought-provoking aluminium sculpture on East Moors near Helmsley, the puzzling Face Stone on Urra Moor, the Captain Cook Monument on Easby Moor, the Elgee Memorial Stone on Loose Howe near Rosedale, the Roman Road on Wheeldale Moor near Goathland, the remarkable Derwent Sea Cut near Hackness, almost forty castles, half-a-dozen abbeys including Ampleforth's modern one full of monks, countless churches and chapels, houses and farms, roads, railways and bridges, along with many memorials, way markers, parish boundary stones and what is probably Britain's largest collection of stone crosses. One of those crosses, (Lilla Cross on Fylingdales Moor) is probably England's oldest Christian relic, dating to AD 626. The stone crosses of the North York Moors are certainly the largest in such a compact area. To these can be added similar structures in the Yorkshire Dales and on the Yorkshire Wolds, but the

Dales and Wolds are a long way from the North Yo
and provide their own range of stories.

One would think that a modest addition to this host of
land complements would not be noticed or that no one would object to such a presence, but in these days of complex building rules and the need for planning permission, plus the inevitable NIMBY (Not In My Back Yard) syndrome, any attempt to erect a new edifice on the moors is bound to be challenged. Such challenges are done on the basis that if you don't like something or don't understand it, you should object to it. There was a similar attitude in the 1960s.

When the three famous white globes of Fylingdale Ballistic Missile Early Warning Station were erected in the early 1960s, there was almighty fuss with lots of vigorous protests but the duck-egg white globes were built in spite of the objections and eventually became a beautiful and romantic sight on our bleak moorland. When they were removed in 1994 to be replaced by a truncated pyramid-type building containing SSPAR (Solid State Phased Array Radar), there were further protests by those who said that the three white globes should remain *in situ* even if they were obsolete. At the very least, the grumblers said, one of them should be retained. But none was, maintenance of such a relic being extremely costly.

The York sculptor, Austin Wright, had similar problems when he placed his controversial aluminium sculpture on the moors above Helmsley in 1977 – there were objections galore and yet the piece is now regarded as an asset to the area while providing a fascinating focal point on those moorland hills, in spite of damage by vandals.

It is not surprising, therefore, that when a Yorkshire sculptor called Haldan Chance applied for planning permission to erect one of his creations on the moors, he expected an avalanche of protests. His proposal was to instal one of his giant, modernistic and rather baffling timber-framed works on the remote Three Howes Rigg, an eminence on the moors above Aidensfield. I had never heard of Haldan Chance before that time and knew nothing of his work; it seems that no one else knew anything about him either because no one was precisely sure what the thing would look like when complete, except that it would be modern, controversial, roughly egg-shaped and built of wood.

In presenting his plans to the planning authorities, Haldan made it clear that he could not provide precisely detailed plans of his creation because its final appearance and style would emerge only while it was being moulded in the middle of that remote, untamed piece of windswept moorland. He did say, however, that it would comprise natural ingredients and would be egg-shaped; to support his application, he produced drawings and photographs of similar works in different parts of the world, ranging from the Himalayas to the jungles of Borneo. He also produced letters from supporters who said they had total faith in his concept – whatever he did produce would be memorable, enduring and important. After all, he was a sculptor of international renown.

One minor problem was that sketches and photographs of his other works, and an outline of this proposal, had never been viewed by the general public. They were seen only by the planners.

News of his rather controversial proposal reached the public when the Press published a summary of his ideas after they had been discussed at a planning meeting of the North York Moors National Park Authority. Due to the powerful support he had secured from the North Riding of Yorkshire Arts Council, coupled with some financial input from several well-known Yorkshire sponsors, his scheme had won the narrowest of approvals. Apparently, someone on the planning committee pointed out that if the government could erect the massive early warning station on a moorland hill at Fylingdales, then surely Haldan Chance could not be prevented from erecting something of a similar but much smaller shape. Whatever the appearance of his egg-shaped creation, it would be but a pimple compared with the might of the early warning station on a neighbouring hilltop – a pipit's egg compared with its three BMEWS ostrich eggs. Against that kind of simple logic, Haldan won his approval.

Following this approval, there were members of the public who thought the planners had lost their brains, especially those whose more conventional plans had been rejected. There were also some subsequent rumblings from feature writers and questioning correspondence from the public in the local Press, but in spite of it all, Haldan set about his task and one of his first actions was to visit me. Having telephoned to make the necessary appointment, he arrived at my police house around noon on a Monday in late spring. I had no idea what he looked like, but he arrived in a beautiful maroon 3.4 litre Jaguar which he drove into my drive and from which he emerged with a brief-case full of sketches and other papers.

I think I expected an artistic-looking character with a beard, jeans and sandals, but this was a tall and very distiguished-looking gentleman in his mid-sixties whose bearing and sheer force of personality suggested he was a member of the aristocracy. With an erect carriage, lots of pure white and very well-cut hair, a white moustache equally well trimmed and very fresh pink skin, he was the epitome of sparkling health, while his lovat green suit was clearly very expensive and tailor-made. He wore highly polished brown brogue shoes too. Without doubt he had the appearance of a well-off Yorkshire landowner and this was reinforced when he spoke with a clipped upper-crust accent; also, I noticed gold rings on the fingers of his left hand and an expensive watch on his wrist. Clearly he was a man of wealth and style.

I led him into my plain office and settled him on a battered police-issue chair while Mary went off to organize some coffee – I hoped she would find a mug without any cracks or chips. Having dispensed with the preliminaries, he said, 'Well, Constable Rhea, I'm sure you'll be wondering why I wanted a chat with you.'

'Yes, your work on the Rigg is hardly a police matter!' I smiled, having read about his enterprise.

'Indeed my work is not, but my rather extended preparatory measures are within your jurisdiction,' he said. 'And for that reason, I need your co-operation.'

He opened his briefcase and placed a pen-and-ink drawing on my desk. Before I could examine it, he followed it with an Ordnance Survey map which he quickly unfolded and spread in front of me.

'That is a preliminary and rather rough sketch of my work, Mr Rhea,' he said, addressing me with some formality. 'I shall start next week, but before I discuss that, I thought I should identify the site of my sculpture to you so there is no doubt in your mind.'

On the map, he pointed to Three Howes Rigg. It was a very remote and exposed place rising to about a thousand feet above sea level with no road leading to the summit, although there were narrow, unsurfaced footpaths to the top from three different locations in the dales below. Totally devoid of trees and shrubs but covered with heather like much of the surrounding moorland, this particular summit was visible from far and wide; the extensive views from the top were stunning with the North Sea being visible to the east and the Pennines to the west, with the lesser dales and villages being spread below like a geographic model. There were views throughout the full 360 degrees as one stood on that site – and that meant that Haldan's sculpture would be visible from a great distance on all sides and from a variety of vantage points upon the lower ground.

I began to wonder what impact it would have upon people who viewed it as they crossed those moors or journeyed through the dales below either on foot, by motor vehicle or train, or even flew over it by aircraft. Whatever its final appearance, it might, from a distance, appear to be a terrible blot on the landscape or an egg-like pimple on the moortop or just another curious object to add to the thousand or so standing stones. At this stage, and in spite of his sketches, I had no notion of the appearance of his finished work.

'I know the Rigg,' I said, adding, 'although I seldom visit the place in the course of my duties. If I do go, it's usually for a long walk in pleasant weather conditions. It's not the sort of place you drop in to see while passing.'

'I think the same could be said of most visitors to the Rigg's summit,' he agreed. 'And I would hope that the presence of my work on that summit would encourage visitors to make the effort to climb the Rigg, either to view it or to involve themselves in it. Now, my reason for coming to see you is to ask you to keep a professional eye on my work as it progresses. I cannot be on the site for twenty-four hours every day and I do need to leave my raw materials and equipment unattended for a considerable time. I do not want them stolen or damaged, you see. That is the purpose of this visit, Constable, to ask you to ensure there is no vandalism to, or theft of, any of my materials or equipment.'

'But it's a two-mile hike to the top of the Rigg!' I said. 'It's not on any of my regular routes. It's not as if I shall be passing frequently! And I doubt if opportunist thieves are likely to be passing either.'

I felt I had to tell this imposing gentleman that I had other duties, and that protection of his raw materials on the isolated hill-top was not my most pressing responsibility.

'But it is your duty to protect property, is it not, Constable?'

As he spoke, I could hear the voice of the aristocracy; I could imagine this man giving orders to a village constable from his country mansion in years gone by and wondered about his background and upbringing.

In this respect he was something of a mystery. I'd never heard of him prior to this development and knew nothing of his background, nor had I seen any of his creations in our galleries or museums. That was not surprising, however, because I was not a regular visitor to art galleries or exhibitions and his work was not the sort which would attract my attention from a professional point of view. As a policeman, I had no formal interest in Haldan Chance. But in listening to him and observing his demeanour, I could imagine Haldan regarding the local constable as a member of his own staff just as some landowners used to do until comparatively recently. And I was not going to allow that to happen.

'I have eight villages to patrol, in addition to extra duties in Ashfordly, Strensford and elsewhere, Mr Chance,' I said. 'But of course I shall pay due attention to your materials. If you tell me where your belongings will be and how they can be identified, I shall ensure that all patrolling police officers know about them. But I cannot guarantee twenty-four hour security, no one can. Nonetheless, I shall personally keep an eye on the site as I undertake the general scope of my other duties.'

'My materials will be on the hill-top.' He looked at me as if I was not comprehending his wishes. 'Everything will be on the Rigg as I work; everything will be up there day and night, Constable, in the open air, unfenced and vulnerable. I need everything to hand as I create my work; I do not want to have to stop in order to obtain a small item. Everything I need will be there and I am sure you will appreciate I cannot produce a work of art if someone has removed any component or vital part or caused damage to them. So, when I have completed a day's work, I shall have to leave the materials behind and that means they will be unattended. I cannot take them with me. I am not like an artist with a paintbrush and easel. I am a sculptor of earth materials. That is my problem.'

'So what in fact are we talking about?' I asked. 'What kind of materials will they be?'

'Wood, Constable. Timber. Tree trunks in fact.'

'Tree trunks?' I was puzzled now.

'And concrete,' he added.

'Concrete?'

'Yes. And in addition to my raw materials, there will be a concrete mixer, along with digging tools, a saw bench and sundry other items, perhaps including some boulders or large stones.'

'It sounds more like a building site to me!' I tried to make light of this but he was deadly serious.

'It is a building site, Constable Rhea, I shall be constructing my work of art, an enduring piece of rural art imbued with the deep symbolism of nature with overtones of history in the past, present and future, and I shall do so with earth materials as I have explained. I know that you and your colleagues patrol building sites to protect them against vandals and thieves, which is precisely what I require at my site. Nothing more, nothing less.'

'The moors up there are private property,' I pointed out. 'Ashfordly Estate owns them and the police therefore have restricted access. Our rights are just the same as those of the general public, which is why large enterprises like factories and department stores employ their own security staff. Our powers are limited in private premises, Mr Chance. I ought to make you aware of that.'

'I do realize that, Constable, for I have been in regular discussion with the estate office, but I will point out that there are public footpaths to the summit. The public is not excluded, Constable, and crimes might be committed.'

'Footpaths, yes, not roads. So how do you propose to convey your large materials and equipment to the site?' I asked.

'I have made arrangements to hire a tractor and trailer,' he said. 'And a saw bench, and a concrete mixer. And I need a device for lifting the tree trunks so that their bases can be guided into the holes I shall prepare. I have spoken to your local timber merchant, a Mr Stone.'

'Well, Mr Chance, I think that if a thief wanted to steal anything, he would have to make similar arrangements, and I cannot see any thief taking the time or trouble to do that, not for a tree trunk or bit of cement. But I will enter your request for supervision in our occurrence book so that all my colleagues are fully aware of the potential vulnerable property. In short, I shall do what I can to protect your property, bearing in mind the constraints.'

'Good, that is what I want to hear. I shall be making a start next Monday morning, which means the materials will be on site from around noon onwards.'

'Thanks,' I said, deciding not to argue any further. 'We'll do our best to safeguard them.'

'Now, Constable Rhea, this is a sketch of the finished work, not even the planners have seen this but I thought you might be interested.' He closed the map to reveal the piece of cartridge paper which was on my desk. It bore a pencil drawing which had been colour-washed in watercolour paint. Although there was no indication of its size, I thought it looked like a tulip flower head sitting on the moor. I decided to express that opinion, knowing that some artists like to ponder the differing views of their public.

'It's like a tulip head,' I said quietly.

'Is that how you see it?' he frowned.

'Or the partially open seed box of some kind of wild flower perhaps,' I added.

'How about an egg?' he suggested.

'Yes,' I had to admit. 'It is rather egg-shaped, albeit with a flat base . . . or perhaps like an orange which has been opened into segments. . . .'

'Good,' he said, beaming at me. 'It's nature, you see. Different people will see different images in my finished work but all, I hope, will express nature in one of its many forms.'

'So how large will it be?' I asked.

'What you have interpreted as petals of the tulip are in fact tree trunks,' he told me. 'Each will be twelve feet high and I shall use twelve of them to form a hollow circle.'

'Tree trunks?' I must have sounded surprised.

'Yes, the very best. They will represent the twelve hours of day, or even the twelve hours of night, or even the twelve months of the year. They might even be seen as the Twelve apostles to someone of a religious frame of mind or the Twelve Tables of Roman law . . . twelve is a very significant figure in our culture, Constable. Now, the bottom of each tree will be set in concrete, and the tops will incline inwards towards each other.'

'Curved trunks?' I registered my surprise.

'Yes, indeed. Curved. Now curved tree trunks are very difficult to obtain, Constable, especially when one requires twelve of an identical size, or as near identical as possible. But I did find them and have already had the trees felled; the wood is awaiting me as we speak. There is a variety of timber as one might expect – ash, oak, sycamore, elm . . . all curved, all green wood. The winds of the moors will dry and season the timber, so it will endure for generations. So this is to be a large and enduring piece of work, Constable Rhea.'

'No one's going to steal those trees in a hurry!' I told him.

'If I can get them to the site, then a determined thief could remove them,' he said seriously.

'We'll keep an eye on things,' I promised.

Thanking me for my assistance, Haldan Chance replaced his drawings and maps, bade me farewell and drove away with a throaty roar from his Jaguar. I thought then that being a sculptor must be a means of growing wealthy.

A couple of days later, I was in Ashfordly Police Station on a routine visit and entered the budding sculpture's details in the occurrence book as I'd promised Haldan. Sergeant Blaketon was having two days off so I had no opportunity to mention this unusual duty to him. It was on the Friday following that he rang me.

'Rhea,' his voice sounded ominous. 'What's this about paying periodic crime-prevention visits to Three Howes Rigg? Isn't that in the middle of nowhere? We are not private security guards, Rhea. Isn't that land on private property? I thought those moors belonged to Ashfordly Estate?'

'They do, Sergeant, but there are public routes to the moors and onto the summit. I explained all that to Mr Chance and he understood the restrictions we face when dealing with matters on private premises.'

'Well if you want to waste your time and energy climbing up there to make sure no one's stolen a tree trunk, then that's up to you, but I am not going to instruct my other officers to do likewise. We have more important things to do with our time, Rhea. Bearing in mind the site is on private land, I think your friend should make his own security arrangements to reinforce the limited supervision we can give.'

'Very good, Sergeant.' I knew better than to argue with my supervisory officer.

It would be about a week later when I received a further telephone call from Sergeant Blaketon.

'Rhea,' he barked into the handset, 'what is that banana

doing on the skyline of Three Howes Rigg?'

'Banana, Sergeant?'

'Well, it looks like a giant banana to me. I thought that thing up there was going to be egg-shaped or tulip-shaped. . .'

'It's all in the eye of the beholder, Sergeant.' I smiled as I talked to him. 'The sculptor expects every viewer to see something different in his work. . . .'

'Yes, I can appreciate that, but you'd never get bananas growing on the North York Moors, Rhea.'

'It's a tree trunk, Sergeant, a curved one but there's just one in position at the moment. When it's finished, there'll be twelve, all curved . . .' I began.

'In which case it will look like a bunch of bananas, Rhea. How did that chap get planning permission for his bananas?'

'Maybe the planners thought it looked like a globe artichoke,' I said. 'Or a grouse chick at rest, or a young mushroom. . . .'

'Whatever it is, it's your problem, Rhea, although I must admit I can't see any ordinary member of the public objecting if someone spirited away that banana at the dead of night.'

It was that remark which reminded me that I had not yet managed to find the time to climb up to Three Howes Rigg in an effort to show the uniform, although conversely Haldan Chance had not reported any trouble.

One quiet day, therefore, I decided to pay a duty call to the sculpture site. As I approached, I could see that six trunks were now standing like the five curved fingers of a human hand – albeit with one extra – the hand being held open palm upwards as if to receive a gift. I drove my Mini-van to within half a mile of the summit – half a mile as the crow flies, that is, and then had to complete a steep, winding climb by using one of the marked footpaths. When I arrived, panting and perspiring, Haldan Chance was already there along with his Land-rover and the accoutrements of a building operation. In his shirt sleeves, he was digging a huge hole to accommodate yet another tree trunk and did not see my approach. Like the others, that tree would be concreted into position. As I grew nearer, it was quite astonishing to see the effect generated by this semi-circle of huge curved tree trunks. As I approached, I found myself admiring the long-distance views through the gaps in the trunks already in position.

'Ah, Constable Rhea,' beamed Haldan Chance as he came towards me, wiping his hand on a rag. 'So, what do you think of it so far?'

'Quite remarkable,' I had to admit. 'Very impressive; much more impressive that I would have thought.'

'Then that pleases me. And there have been no thefts or damage,' he said. 'Thanks for your attention.'

'I had a few minutes on hand today,' I told him, without revealing that this was my first visit. 'So I thought I would come along to see how you were progressing.'

'It's a slow process,' he said. 'Very laborious too, tough and hard manual labour, not like painting a picture, for example. I can't manage to manhandle the trunks, they're far too heavy and cumbersome, so I need Mr Stone's machinery to lift them into the holes, like they do with telegraph poles, and that costs money and time . . . but I'm getting there. This trunk is number seven. Any comments from the village?'

'My sergeant says it looks like a bunch of bananas,' I smiled.

'One man I spoke to said it was like a group of stooped old folks having a chat among themselves,' he grinned. 'And another thought it was like a flame of some kind rising from the ground. Amazing, eh? I never cease to be amazed at the interpretations people place on my work. But that is precisely its purpose, to make people think about things.'

We talked for a few minutes, but I could see that he wanted to complete some of the base concrete work before his current supply hardened in the mixer which chugged nearby; at this closer range, the growing sculpture was truly like a building site and yet it had this remarkable effect to look so different in the eyes of individuals. I left Haldan to his curious work and returned home.

Eventually, all twelve tree trunks were in position and the site machinery was removed by Haldan. His sculpture was complete and he left without saying farewell to me. But his creation remained – from the valleys below and from all the surrounding hilltops and moorland summits, everyone could see the spectacle.

And, as Haldan had predicted, people began to trek to the summit during the summer months. They wanted to see what his sculpture was like at close quarters. Some of the visitors merely walked past while others explored the tall ring of tree trunks; some had picnics within the circle, while others used it as a place for a romantic rendezvous. Photographs were taken for private and commercial purposes while artists came to paint pictures. Within the space of a few months, the place had become a focus for all kinds of activities which were undertaken by a wide range of people, young and old, local and visitor alike. One travel writer even called the site Tree Howes Rigg instead of Three Howes Rigg, but those of us who read it wondered if it was an understandable mistake.

There is no doubt the sculpture was a success, but during the summer I had a visit from our local timber merchant, Paddy Stone.

'You met that sculptor chap, didn't you, Nick?' he began, as I seated him before my desk. 'The chap who built that thing on Three Howes. Haldan Chance.'

'Yes, briefly,' I agreed. 'Is there a problem?'

'Well, he's not paid me for the hire of my lifting equipment. Or those tree trunks I found for him. They took me a long time, finding a dozen matching trunks. . . .'

'I'm afraid that's a civil debt, Paddy,' I had to tell him. 'It's not a police matter.'

'Well I think the police should take an interest. I reckon he was a con merchant,' Paddy continued. 'I've had words with the National Park people because I'd heard he never paid for the holiday cottage he rented at Milthorpe while he was applying for his grants and planning permission while he was working on that tree thing. And he hasn't paid the garage for the petrol he used in that Jag of his. . . .'

And Paddy then related to me a string of unpaid debts left by

Haldan Chance – petrol at the garage, food at the shop, a telephone bill at the holiday cottage, a drinks bill in the pub, the hire of a Land-rover and a tractor and trailer, hardware such as tools and cement from a builders' merchants . . . . according to Paddy, Haldan Chance had not paid for anything and yet he had received a series of grants to enable him to complete his artistic creation. That money was supposed to be sufficient to pay for his materials and other expenses and also to provide him with some payment for the work. It began to look as if this was a police matter; instead of being what we described as an unsatisfactory business transaction, Haldan's behaviour now seemed to have the flavour of a confidence trick. If he was a confidence trickster, however, he was a very clever one.

In an attempt to discover more about this mysterious sculptor, I drove into Ashfordly for a meeting with Alan Cook, the finance director of the National Park Authority. Although the park itself had not suffered financially, Mr Cook did say he'd had several complaints about Haldan, chiefly from people and businesses who were trying to trace him following non-payment of their accounts.

The snag was no one could trace Haldan Chance – he'd vanished as suddenly as he had arrived. Mr Cook told me he'd spoken to an official of the North Riding of Yorkshire Arts Council who admitted Haldan Chance was unknown to them, but his grant from the council had resulted from his portfolio of works, pictures of which suggested he was a sculptor of worldwide renown. But, it seems, a careful check by experts on the source of those pictures had shown them to be the work of other sculptors – and no one had spotted the deception until the manifestation of recent worries about Haldan. It seems he had used the holiday cottage, on a long let, as his address while negotiating his grants and planning permission. And now, the bird had flown from his nest.

I next drove to Milthorpe for a chat with the owner of Millstone Cottage, a Mr Jim Brownlow. His description of Haldan Chance was perfect and it matched the memories of him which I retained, but Haldan had not paid paid one penny of rent for his occupancy. Brownlow had regarded him as a perfect country gentleman – he left the place neat and tidy but owing eight months rent.

Although I was gradually uncovering a catalogue of false pretences by Haldan Chance, none of his victims would make a formal crime complaint. Even Paddy Stone refused to make an official complaint to the police – all he wanted was Haldan's address so he could chase him for the monies due. But no one knew his address or his current whereabouts – indeed, no one knew where he had come from in the first place.

I spoke to Sergeant Blaketon about this and his attitude was that unless someone came forward to register an official complaint about a crime, e.g. false pretences or obtaining credit by fraud, then we could not take any formal action to trace and prosecute Haldan Chance. He suggested I revisit his victims with a view to securing at least one formal complaint, but no one would consent to that – they did not want Haldan brought before a criminal court; all they wanted was their money.

Haldan Chance was never traced and I never saw another reference to him. Some said he had built his tree sculpture on the moors as a joke, or to draw attention to the silly things which were regarded as art, but whatever their feelings, he did obtain cash for it and he did build it.

The odd thing is that Haldan's sculpture continues to occupy its hill-top site on Three Howes Rigg above Aidensfield. It is much weathered now, but it has endured storms, snowdrifts and vandalism along with the constant carving of lovers' initials, children using it as a climbing frame and adults adapting it as an over-night camping-site or temporary shelter with tarpaulins stretched across the top. It has even survived a moorland fire because its wide concrete base and the patch of bare moorland which surrounds it, combined to keep the wind-driven flames at bay. There is no doubt it is a well-built structure, the combined work of man and nature.

Whatever Haldan's intention, his work of art has survived and it is now a permanent feature of our dramatic landscape. Sometimes I wonder what he would think of that – and sometimes I wonder if he (or his spirit) has ever returned to admire the views from the inside and outside of those twelve curved tree trunks.

While the Haldan Chance stockade on Three Howes Rigg did not cause a great deal of inconvenience from a police point of view, the same could not be said about a set of illuminated metal pillars which appeared on the main street in Ashfordly, our local market town. For some weeks after their installation at the High Street/Brantsford Street crossroads, they caused absolute mayhem among pedestrians and traffic alike whereas they were designed to do precisely the opposite. They were supposed to aid the flow of through-traffic, prevent congestion and allow pedestrians to cross the street in relative safety. These magic pillars were, in fact, the town's first set of traffic lights and they replaced a succession of policemen who had to perform long sessions of arm-aching traffic duty at those crossroads. The problem was that most drivers ignored them at first or failed to understand their message, although in time, having grown accustomed to policemen standing in the middle of the road while behaving like windmills, they became accustomed to this new and highly advanced form of traffic control.

Few motorists living on the moors and in the surrounding market towns had had any experience with traffic lights; indeed, few had ever had to negotiate a roundabout or a pedestrian crossing, consequently, strange additions of this kind, which were to be found only in town and city streets, created bewilderment in the minds of rural drivers. Drivers from country areas are accustomed to making up their own minds on matters such as when to stop and start, when to turn left or right, where to park or when to hurtle over a crossroads.

Having been nurtured into making their own decisions about most things, they did not take kindly to a set of coloured lights which took away some of their decision-making functions. To their credit, of course, the drivers on the moors were amazingly skilled at negotiating the steepest of gradients, the sharpest of corners, the most difficult of reversing requirements, the longest of flocks of sheep, the deepest of snowdrifts, the iciest of road surfaces, the muddiest of lanes or the most watery of flooded fords, but artificial highway controls like traffic lights, roundabouts and pedestrian crossings did tend to baffle them.

I think a lot of rural drivers did not regard these controls as something to be permanently obeyed – some thought they existed only for use in difficult times and so, if a traffic light showed red when there was nothing else on the road, it was usually ignored. In the mind of a rural motorist, it did not make sense to stop when there was no other traffic on the road. And why trouble to go completely around a roundabout by driving to the left when a short, sharp acceleration to the right would put you on the road you desired?

Among this army of perplexed rural drivers was one Amos Burnley, a crusty, short-tempered 85-year-old bachelor who lived at Lingmoor House, Aidensfield. A retired accountant who enjoyed a few glasses of sherry and a whisky or two, he was a tall, rather stooped gentleman who dressed in a somewhat shabby manner in one of a plentiful supply of old tweed sports jackets with ragged sleeves and leather-patched elbows worn with unpressed cavalry twill trousers in varying shades of brown.

He ran a beautiful bottle-green Riley car with a long bonnet and a black roof. but unfortunately his driving skills had been learned many years earlier on near-deserted roads. Consequently, whenever he wanted to go anywhere, he simply aimed his car and launched it, rather like a guided missile. He was always completely unaware of other traffic either in front or behind him. The people of Aidensfield were keenly aware of his rather idiosyncratic driving and coped quite simply by keeping out of his way. One thing which helped in this was his regular behaviour – he always went to the bank at the same time of the day, he posted his letters, did his shopping and performed every other necessary function at set times each day or week. Thus the people of Aidensfield knew his routine and ensured they were off the streets as he was taking off in the Riley.

One of his more renowned and alarming habits was to drive

over crossroads and out of junctions without taking heed of any other approaching vehicle. Amos seemed to think he had a permanent right of way in all cases. When such intersections were deserted, there was no problem, but when other vehicles were approaching whose drivers knew *they* had the right of way, the outcome was often a noisy and alarming few moments of severe braking by them, some urgent steering-wheel manipulation followed by a car or two in the hedge or ditch accompanied by much rending of metal, breaking of glass, muttering and swearing. The final act in these oft-repeated rural dramas was the sight of Amos's Riley disappearing into the distance. That always happened – he was never in a collision and the bodywork of his old car was as perfect as the day it was built.

Without fail, he and his car escaped unscathed whereas his driving had put other cars out of action in the ditch, or sometimes in the garage for repairs to bodywork and paintwork. Occasionally, his driving put other drivers in the care of a nurse or doctor, but happily, there were never any serious casualties and, oddly enough, he had never been charged with any serious driving offence. The locals rarely reported their minor mishaps with Amos; I think they regarded them as an acceptable part of their daily lives, as much their fault as his, and from time to time, he offered to pay for minor repairs. I think such acts kept him out of court.

In police terms, however, each time such an incident happened, Amos had caused an accident – the Road Traffic Act of 1960 legislated for traffic accidents by saying 'If, owing to the presence of a motor vehicle on a road, an accident occurs.' . . . It is not necessary that the offending vehicle actually suffers a collision – merely by being on the road where its presence causes an accident is sufficient for it to be regarded as involved' – and that scenario fitted Amos precisely. There is no doubt that, over the years, Amos's green Riley had caused dozens of accidents even if it had never suffered a scratch or a dent.

In addition to an offence of failing to stop after a road accident or failing to report an accident, Amos might be guilty of careless or even dangerous driving, or driving without reasonable consideration for other road users. Somehow, though, he had evaded all such prosecutions. It was with this knowledge in mind that I wondered how he would cope with Ashfordly's new traffic lights – he was of the age where he would halt at a policeman's signal, but traffic lights were not human.

Amos did not often drive into Ashfordly, however, which was perhaps a good thing, although it was unfortunate that the lights became operative only three weeks before Christmas. For the police officers of Ashfordly this was indeed a welcome Christmas present because it removed the need for a cold, wet constable to be on regular traffic duty. Prior to the arrival of the lights, we had all taken our turn in performing traffic control duties at those crossroads. We had to stand in the middle of the crossroads at busy times – 8 a.m. to 9 a.m. each weekday morning, 4.45 p.m. to 5.45 p.m. each weekday evening and all day Saturday and Sunday during the peak holiday periods when tourists and coaches passed this way *en route* to the coast. It was an arm-aching chore, and it removed us from other necessary or more urgent duties. Even if there was murder and mayhem in town, we had to stand there and keep the traffic moving. But now it was all over. The marvels of modern mechanization had taken over this unwelcome duty.

The traffic lights arrived at a time when the nights and even the days were dark and when the weather had a tendency to produce rain, sleet and even some soggy snowflakes. During those first few days of life for the new lights, as they performed their non-stop colour-changing routine, the wet snow did not lie, but it meant the roads and atmosphere were in a state of permanent dampness. Driving on wet roads is never easy, particularly in small towns where the lights of the shops and streets reflect from the damp surface.

I was to learn that Amos's first post-traffic-light venture in Ashfordly occurred one Thursday evening, only two days after they'd been switched on.

They were showing red as he approached them around 5 p.m. that evening, but, true to form, he did not stop. He sailed into the crossroads as if there was no other car on the road. But there was; in fact, there were lots because this was one of the small town's busiest times. To avoid Amos and his car, an oncoming but empty delivery van, slammed into the wall of a nearby shop, a pick-up rammed into the rear of a saloon car which stopped suddenly, a car driven by a company representative swerved and mounted the footpath, causing a man to leap for his life into the doorway of the nearby bank where he pushed his elbow through the glass panelling of the closed door, while a motor cyclist skidded on the wet road surface before falling into the path of a bus. The bus crushed his bike but he escaped with bruises. A pedestrian raced for safety dropping her shopping all over the road and someone said a cat had fled for its life too. And old Amos, in his green Riley, motored sedately away without stopping and without a scratch. But someone took his registration number and reported it to Ashfordly Police where Sergeant Blaketon learned of the incident.

He rang me.

'Go and see this maniac!' he instructed me in no uncertain terms. 'Interview him and tell him he's being reported for failing to stop after an accident and you might care to add a careless driving charge, Rhea.'

I explained that Aidensfield drivers knew about Amos and his foibles, but that did not appease Blaketon who growled, 'Well, if he can't cope with modern traffic, it's time he was put off the road, Rhea. He sounds to be something of a menace, a danger to himself and others. Let's hope the court orders him to take a driving test or eyesight test, or perhaps his insurance company will refuse to cover him. . . .'

When I went to interview Amos at his beautiful home, he invited me in and then offered me a dry sherry. As it was approaching Christmas, I accepted, while stressing I was here to report him for several possible driving offences; the sherry could not prevent me from doing my duty and he said he fully understood that. His offer of a drink was due to his excellent manners, not any attempt to offer a bribe. I explained the reason for my presence and after a while I saw him frown.

'Traffic lights?' he puzzled. 'What traffic lights, Mr Rhea?'

'In Ashfordly High Street, Mr Burnley. They've just been installed at the crossroads.'

'Well, I never saw them.' He shook his head. 'I know that one has to stop when the light shows red. I am not stupid, you know, or ignorant of traffic rules and regulations. There's usually a policeman on duty there, I always stop for him if he raises his hand. I was brought up to obey policemen, Mr Rhea, but I never saw one. So how long have the lights been there?'

I explained they were a very recent addition to the street furnishings of Ashfordly, but he shook his head and said, 'I saw only Christmas lights, Mr Rhea, lights of all colours flashing and shining in the darkness, shop lights, street lights, Christmas-tree lights in shops, shop-window lights, green, red, orange. . . .'

I recorded this piece of mitigation in the statement I took down at his dictation and felt it had some merit. After all, on a wet night there would be lots of reflected lights in a town street and to some extent, I sympathied with Amos, but I could not ignore what had occurred. It was for a court to decide his future after considering all the circumstances.

'Will you be going through Ashfordly again?' I asked, when I had completed my interview, having also inspected his driving licence, excise duty disc and insurance.

'Oh yes,' he smiled. 'Every Thursday evening. An old friend has come to live at Slemmington and we have agreed to have a rendezvous at his house every Thursday at five-thirty, for cocktails and a chat, followed by supper. So I shall be motoring through Ashfordly quite regularly, Mr Rhea, and I expect I shall see a lot of him over Christmas and the New Year.'

'Well, just remember those traffic lights and stop if they show red!'

'Yes, of course, Mr Rhea.'

I submitted my report to Sergeant Blaketon who would forward it to the superintendent for a decision as to whether or not Amos should be prosecuted, but on this occasion, due to his assertion about being confused by the multi-coloured lights of the town and the fact the traffic lights were a very new installation, the superintendent decided to issue a written caution.

Perhaps the proximity of Christmas made him a little more charitable than usual. But the following Thursday at 5 p.m. the same thing happened.

A smart, unidentified motor car shot through the lights at red and caused two lorries to meet head-on, a cyclist to hurtle on to the footpath and into the arms of a passing pedestrian and a bus to swerve into the bollards of a traffic island. The bus driver was the same one who'd experienced Amos's daring drive earlier and, although he felt it was the same car, he could not prove it was as he'd not had the time to note its number. Everyone thought Amos had passed that way, but no one could prove it.

Blaketon rang me.

'Rhea, it appears that man of yours has been causing traffic mayhem again. Can you persuade him to take another route to see his old pal?'

'There is no other route, Sergeant, he has to pass through Ashfordly.'

'Then get him to take a taxi or a bus, or walk or something. I don't want this kind of problem every Thursday night at rush hour!'

'Are you sure it was Amos, Sergeant?' I smiled as I asked this question, something I was able to do if I was on the telephone to him.

'Sure? That bus driver is sure even if he didn't get the number. . . .'

'I think we should make sure it is him before I revisit him to accuse him of dangerous driving or some such offence,' I suggested.

'Right, Rhea, a brilliant idea! So, next Thursday, you will perform traffic duty at those crossroads. You will watch out for your Mr Burnley and you will note any offences he might commit. . . .'

'Traffic duty, Sergeant? But we've got traffic lights there now. . . .'

'Then you will have to operate in conjunction with the lights, Rhea. Just make sure that man does not cause mayhem in my town!'

That particular Thursday was the one before Christmas and so, at 4.45 p.m. that evening, with the drizzle falling and the air as cold as the inside of a refrigerator, I stood at those crossroads. I did not compete with the lights, of course, but I stood on the footpath awaiting the arrival of Amos in his Riley. Then I would leap into the road and exercise my arms as I guided him through the traffic.

Sure enough, he was as prompt as always and I saw the distinctive vehicle heading my way. I went into the middle of the road and raised my white-gloved hand; Amos stopped, as did the other traffic. I checked that the lights were working and when I saw the green light glow as the signal for Amos to proceed, I waved my hand in the Highway Code's finest 'come on' sign. He smiled, waved in acknowledgement and executed the necessary right turn without a hitch. Then, with a toot of his horn, he accelerated off to visit his pal. I retreated from the crossroads and allowed the lights to assume control, deciding not to wait until Amos made his return journey. By then, of course, traffic would be lighter and the risks fewer.

Before returning home, I called at Ashfordly Police Station to inform Sergeant Blaketon of the successful outcome of that mission and he was delighted.

'So, Rhea, we got old Amos through those lights without a hitch. Nice work. Nice accident prevention work, in fact. So do it again next Thursday and the Thursday after. . . .'

'Sarge?' I began to protest. 'But there's traffic lights; we can't afford the time to stand there just for Amos, not when we've had brand new lights installed. . . .'

'It's either that, Rhea, or risk the possibility of having to deal with multiple traffic accidents every Thursday evening, to say nothing of complaints from other drivers! Risk limitation, Rhea, that's what it is. Risk limitation. Our duties do include prevention of offences and the protection of the public, as you fully realize. That is what we are doing.'

And so, every Thursday over that Christmas and into January, either me or one of my colleagues had to perform a short bout of traffic duty at those crossroads, just as we had done for all those years in the past, but I am sure we did prevent a lot of accidents which would have been caused by Amos and his car. On those occasions, he obeyed all our manual signals without question and without mishap, and we had no further trouble from him – not on that corner, anyway.

Then, one Thursday in late January, he did not arrive at the crossroads as expected. As I was the constable on duty at the time, I missed Amos and was somewhat relieved he had not embarked on the trip, but then, knowing of his finicky mode of life, I became worried.

I told Sergeant Blaketon that Amos had not turned up, to which he replied, 'Then he's probably learned a bit of sense but you'd better be there next week, just in case . . .' and with that advice, I motored home. On the way, I called at Amos's house but there was no one in, and so I stopped at the village shop for a word with Joe Steel.

'He's in hospital, Nick,' Joe told me. 'A traffic accident. It happened this morning in Strensford.'

'A traffic accident? Is he badly hurt?' was my next question.

'Not according to Nurse Margot,' he smiled. 'He's got mild whiplash injuries to his neck and some severe bruising. But he's not in any danger, in spite of his age.'

'So what happened?' I continued.

'He stopped at some traffic lights in Strensford,' smiled Joe. 'And someone ran into him from behind!'

'I don't believe it!' I laughed. 'I didn't think he ever stopped at traffic lights!'

'Well, he has now and look what happened! I wouldn't think he'll want to stop again! Anyway they reckon he'll be home by the weekend; he has a niece who'll be coming to look after him for a day or two.'

Amos came home by ambulance with a support around his neck and, apart from some bruises about his body, he was not badly injured, even if his pride was shaken. I decided I would visit him as a show of friendship and he invited me into his lounge while asking his niece, Margaret, to bring us all a dry sherry. As I waited, he outlined the accident, saying he'd learned to read the signals at traffic lights and fully understood the sequence of the colours. On this occasion, he had pulled up at the lights at the end of the bridge in Strensford and almost immediately, a motorist had rammed him from behind, crushing the boot of his splendid old car and giving him a nasty whiplash injury – which could have been worse. He considered himself lucky.

'That is my very first road accident, Mr Rhea. It has ruined my record of good driving. So, rather than risk my life in the future, I've decided to give up my licence,' he said eventually. 'After all, I am heading for my eighty-sixth birthday and I don't want to die just yet. Certainly, I have no wish to die in a road accident, not after such a long, accident-free record! I'm not badly off, I can always afford to get a taxi or find someone to drive me if I want to go out. So there you are, one motorist less for you to worry about.'

'I'm pleased you've decided to give up your licence,' I said. 'You've had one or two near misses lately and traffic is getting heavier and cars are moving a lot faster. Your generation must find it difficult to cope. . . .'

'Oh, it's not my own driving ability that concerns me,' he said in all seriousness. 'I've never had an accident in my life, Mr Rhea, not until this one, and that was not my fault. No, it's those other lunatics on the road that worry me. I feel I'm not safe these days . . . I mean, Mr Rhea, if people can run into you when you're parked at traffic lights, heaven knows what might happen on the open road. So, to avoid all those bad drivers and to prolong my life for a few more years, I'm going to get off the roads and leave them free to all those fools who cause accidents!'

'A very wise decision,' I said with all honesty.

7

The bigots of the iron time
Had call'd his harmless art a crime.
Sir Walter Scott (1771–1832)

From time to time, police officers encounter people who commit criminal acts without realizing that their behaviour constitutes an offence. Extreme examples are those who steal from open displays in shops; some regard shoplifting as a challenge or a game rather than a crime, but, at the very least, shoplifting is theft with a maximum sentence of ten years' imprisonment. In some circumstances, it could even be classified as burglary which carries fourteen years' imprisonment. On one occasion in my police service, I came across a doting mother whose son repeatedly and illegally 'borrowed' motor cars from parking areas for what has now become known as joy-riding, but she did not believe this was wrong because, as she said, 'The insurance will pay.'

At the other end of the scale are those whose mental capacity is such that they do not understand the real difference between right and wrong. This is something for which our legal system makes allowances while, on the other hand, the legislature creates what are known as 'absolute offences'. This name is given to offences for which there is no excuse! Many motoring offences fit into this category. Exceeding the speed limit in a motor vehicle is one example – there is no point in a driver saying he or she did not realize it was a restricted area or that the speedometer was unknowingly giving a false reading. Either you are speeding or you are not; there are no buts, ifs and wherefores. Similarly, there is no point claiming your motor car insurance policy expired without your knowledge – driving a motor vehicle on a road without a valid certificate of insurance is an absolute offence. There are no excuses. It would be possible to list many similar illegalities, but it is this firm aspect of the law which, from time to time, creates a dilemma within a police officer. In coping with these absolute offences, allowances must sometimes be made by the police and there are times that discretion has to be exercised – an example might be catching a total stranger driving the wrong way down a badly signed one-way street, catching a man breaking the speed limit while rushing his pregnant wife to hospital for an impending birth, or discovering a motorist who has failed to sign his or her driving licence, an act which validates the document. Does a sympathetic constable allow these offenders to be let off with a verbal caution, or should the full weight of the law be thrown at them? It is a matter of the moment for the constable who deals with these matters; how to deal with these minor infringements of the law is left to his discretion. And so it should be. Happily, that privilege remains with a constable – we are not yet a police state, although I recall one socialist politician in the 1960s who wanted the police to exercise no discretion at all in any instance. He wanted the full weight of the law to be implemented in every case . . . and that's dangerous thinking. It would produce a police state.

It was this kind of problem that faced me in dealing with the curious case of John Frederick Chorley, a 17-year-old farm-worker. He lived and worked with his parents, Jack and Janet, at Stone Beck Farm, Whemmelby, and was an only child. John was born rather late into their lives. Both were over forty when he appeared on the scene and thus he found himself reared in a somewhat lonely world with parents who were almost old enough to be his grandparents. If their education and worldly experience were perhaps rather limited, they were loving and caring, and they were immensely proud that they had a son who would eventually inherit the farm. For that reason, they spent a lot of time and energy in helping John to understand the wealth of knowledge needed to run such a business – everything from simple accountancy and commerce to basic veterinary practices, via grassland care and current Ministry of Agriculture regulations and requirements were part of his work. He had to know a little about a lot – and for an uneducated lad, that was not easy. But he did try. One of his parents' schemes was to make him responsible for several pigs, sheep and cows, learning how to care for them, breed from them and sell their offspring at market, and to ensure he covered his costs and made a profit. I have no doubt young John gained a lot of benefit from those practical lessons.

Stone Beck Farm was a large unit with a spacious house and lots of outbuildings. The spread covered an extensive area of open moorland as well as some lush fields in the dale. In addition to his hard-working son, Jack employed a couple of other hands, in addition to taking on extra men at sheep-shearing time, harvest or other busy periods, and there is no doubt he was a popular, hard-working and much-respected farmer.

Likewise, his wife was always busy, rearing poultry, piglets, lambs and calves on the farm and taking an active part in many village organisations such as the Womens' Institute, chapel and parish council. It was a busy, happy household but totally unsophisticated, and I enjoyed my quarterly visits when I had to check their stock registers or when I made unscheduled calls simply because I happened to be patrolling the vicinity. Whenever I arrived and whatever the reason, Janet would always produce a massive chunk of apple pie or gingerbread and cheese or home-made scones with home-made butter, and we would sit for a few minutes at the scrubbed kitchen table over a cup of tea or coffee, sometimes with John, Jack and one of their sheepdogs present, sometimes without them if they were working on the moors or in the fields.

Generally, however, young John always contrived to keep out of my way. I gained the impression that he was uncomfortable in the presence of a uniformed policeman, something quite normal for a lively, uncultured youth of seventeen. I knew him, of course. A tall, strong youth with a shy smile, broad shoulders and the powerful limbs of a working farm-lad, he had long brown hair which generally looked unkempt, but his face was fresh and his grey eyes were bright. Usually, he wore rough clothes which could never be described as fashionable, and he had an old motor bike which he used to ride in from Whemmelby to meet his pals or to attend Saturday night dances in Ashfordly. He attended a lot of motor cycle scramble events on the moors, and sometimes went into Scarborough or Middlesbrough to dances or night clubs with other friends, one of whom had a car.

In addition to these outings, he spent time in Aidensfield, playing billiards and snooker in the village hall, watching cricket or football matches and even visiting the pub if he thought I wouldn't throw him out. But so long as he did not *purchase* intoxicants, there was no reason why he should not visit the pub with his pals. My own belief was that if such youngsters were in the pub, I knew where they were and what they were doing; that was far better than roaming the streets and becoming vandals.

For all his shyness in my company, I never considered John Frederick to be a troublemaker or even a lad who might occasionally overstep the mark so far as the law was concerned. He had strict parents who ensured he behaved himself and it is fair to say he had never given me a moment's concern.

Then, one afternoon, I paid my usual visit for signing their stock register. Both Jack and John were in the fields, so Janet organized a mug of tea for me, along with a plate of fresh buttered scones and strawberry jam. This was indeed a feast, but for her menfolk, it was a mere snack. As I settled down to enjoy it while checking the entries in the stock register, she settled before me at the opposite side of the table and waited in silence until I appended my signature in the appropriate place in the book.

'So, how's things?' I made small talk while finishing my tea and scones.

'There's summat I want to ask while you're here,' Janet said in her slow moorland voice, her dark eyes looking just a little worried. 'I've asked other folks who've not been much help and

I've had words with t'lectric board, but they're no good either.'

'Well, if I can help, I will.' I wondered what I was about to hear.

'It's my 'lectric bill,' she said. 'It's gone sky high this last two or three quarters and I can't fathom it out.'

'You've spoken to the electricity board, have you?' was my first response.

'Oh, aye, Mr Rhea. I had words with one of their chaps and he said if our meter was showing we'd used all that power, then we'd used it and we'd have to pay up.'

'So are those bills much higher than usual?'

'Eight or nine times higher, Mr Rhea.'

'As much as that? Have you bought some extra equipment? Farm equipment, milking machines, electric fires, an immersion heater, cooker, electric radiators, that sort of thing?'

'I've been through all that with those 'lectric chaps,' she sighed. 'Trouble is, we've bought nowt extra this last six months, and that's when my bills have rocketed.'

This problem, while not being a police matter nor part of my official duties, was typical of the role a rural policeman had to play. People, especially those living in outlying districts, had no one else from whom to seek advice, and so we rural bobbies tended to play the part of adviser, friend and counsellor in many cases. This was such an example. Mrs Chorley had probably exhausted every possible avenue in her quest for an explanation to her dilemma, and having been unsuccessful, now turned to the local constable.

'It sounds as if something powerful has been left switched on all the time,' I suggested. 'Does Jack check his buildings before he knocks off for the day?'

'Every night; especially now I've asked him to be careful. But he's got his own meters for t'farm buildings, it's t'house supply I'm talking about. That meter of ours is fair whizzing around, Mr Rhea, clocking up unit after unit.'

As she spoke, I was aware of one old dodge with power supplies. Some characters, with a good working knowledge of electricity, would illegally tap into the supply of other people.

Only a few months earlier, a man with a shed at the bottom of his garden had managed to tap into the supply to a neighbour's house, and thus the neighbour had, for some time, being unwittingly paying for that fellow's heating, lighting and power. Another man in a city had been able to secretly tap into the electricity supply to a street lamp outside his house, thus getting the town council to pay his power bills. Now, I wondered if something similar was happening here. It was to counter such behaviour that the Larceny Act of 1916 had created the specific offence of 'fraudulently abstracting, diverting or using any electricity', and so I found myself having to undertake a small enquiry to see whether that crime was being committed at Stone Beck Farm.

'Could anyone nearby – neighbour, camper, workshop, holiday cottage or such – be tapping into your supply?' I put to her.

'When we had t'lectric chap out to look round t'house, he thought of that and did a check, Mr Rhea. There's nobody pinching 'lectric from our cables, I'm sure of that and he's sure of that, so he said.'

'So how about showing me your meter? Is it still whizzing round now?'

'Aye, going like merry hell, but I'm damned if I can find a reason. Come and see for yourself.'

The meter was in what Janet called the scullery and I studied it briefly before saying, 'Well, it does appear to be going at a fairly rapid rate, but I've no idea how this compares with your normal consumption.'

'Right,' she said. 'If I switch everything off, you'll see it still keeps going. So follow me, Mr Rhea, and watch me switch everything off, one by one. Right round t'house.'

And so I found myself following Janet Chorley around the house, upstairs and downstairs. She switched off everything and unplugged everything that was plugged in, including the radio, all the kitchen equipment, the television set, several standard lamps, the oven, the washing machine and all the lights. I followed her upstairs where she repeated the procedure, unplugging bedside lights, a radio/alarm clock, her hair drier and an electric fire. In young John's room, there was a tangle of wires from a socket, these feeding his record player and own bedside light and an alarm clock, and so she unplugged all those. We even went outside to the wash-house and garage, then checked the greenhouse, but none of the domestic outbuildings was connected either to the domestic power or the business line.

'He uses a fair bit of 'lectric with his records,' she said later. 'And when it's chilly, he plugs a fire in. He spends a fair bit of time in his room these days, there's nowt for a lad of his age up here so I never grumble. He's taken to growing things in t'greenhouse an' all, but that's got no power or light. He uses an oil heater if he needs extra warmth and a storm lantern if he has to check things at night.'

'Keen on gardening, is he?' I asked.

'He's got a lot keener this last few months,' she said. 'I've seen cabbages, sprouts and cauliflowers there, all young plants he's grown from seed. He sells 'em, flowers an' all, for bedding. Don't ask me what they are, I'm no good with flowers.'

'A way of making a bit of pocket money?'

'Aye, we like him to earn a bit extra if he can. He buys records with the money, he likes pop music, you know. He saved up and bought that record player, and his radio and all them records. And his motor bike. All from his gardening, Mr Rhea. He says he wants to buy a smart car next, but he'll have a job saving up enough for that out of his cabbages and things.'

'It won't do him any harm to try. It's good to see him able to make his own amusement and earn a bit of pocket money with it. So, we've been in all the rooms, have we?' I asked. 'Is there any place we've not visited? Anywhere that might have a power socket of some kind?'

'Nay, you've seen t'lot,' she said. 'Every room where we had t'lectric installed. We've no electric anywhere else in t'spot. Now, you done what t'lectric man did, unplugged everything in every room but left t'mains on. He checked t'whole house just like you. Now come and see t'meter.'

She was right. The meter's internal mechanism was continuing to turn as if something requiring a lot of power was switched on and in use.

'You're sure the power lines for the machinery in the buildings haven't somehow got connected to the domestic supply?' I suggested.

'That's what t'lectric man thought, but we checked. You can go down there and see for yourself, you can switch everything off at t'outbuildings' mains.'

'Do you mind if I do that? Then I can go and have words with the Electricity Board in Strensford and tell them what I've seen. If I'm not satisfied about this, I could then ask them to conduct a very thorough examination on the grounds that I suspect a fraudulent abstraction of electricity by someone not connected with the farm.'

'Right,' she said. 'At least summat's getting done.'

Again, she was right. When we isolated the farm buildings by switching off their mains supply, the meter in her house continued to turn as if something was using electricity. As a final check, I switched off her mains supply, and this action did halt the meter. In my mind, it suggested either that some piece of apparatus in the house was faulty and consuming power even though I'd seen everything switched off, or that someone had managed to abstract electricity from the farmhouse supply by a secret means yet to be determined. But now, with confidence, I could speak to someone in authority at the Electricity Board offices in Strensford. I explained my plan to Janet and said I would keep her informed of my progress.

The following morning I called at the Electricity Board offices and found myself speaking to the manager, a Mr Christopher Carson. After explaining my purpose and outlining my experience at Stone Beck Farm, he smiled rather ruefully.

'We've spent a lot of time there, Mr Rhea, checking the farmhouse and the outbuildings, but there's no illegal connection, nor has the farm machinery been inadvertently connected to the domestic supply. We have installed a new meter, just in case the previous one was faulty and it continues to record consumption at what Mrs Chorley believes to be a very high rate. But facts are facts, Mr Rhea. Someone at the farmhouse is using electricity and the meter is recording that fact. It is as simple as that. She pays for the power that goes into that house.'

'But when I switched everything off, the meter continued to operate,' I told him. 'Surely that indicates a problem?'

'I agree that it does suggest something is using power, but we found nothing. We searched the house, just as you did, every room, every nook and cranny, and we found nothing. Even the new meter does that – and we must charge the Chorleys for the consumption that it registers.'

'Are you saying they have something hidden away, something that's using the power and that they are trying to avoid payment?' I put to him.

'Such things are not unknown, Mr Rhea. We rely on our very sophisticated and accurate equipment. In our view, Mr Rhea, the Chorley farm house is using all that electricity. How it does so when everything is apparently switched off, is something of a mystery, but when it comes to avoiding payment for consumption of power, or making claims for reimbursements when the costs are abnormally high, we are alert to every dodge in the book. The onus rests on the householders to prove we are at fault, and they can't do that. Our records are accurate and well tested.'

'I don't think these are dishonest people,' I had to say. 'I truly believe there is a problem. Surely, Mrs Chorley would not involve me, a policeman, if the family was fiddling in some obscure way?'

'Then let's say we agree to differ, Mr Rhea. Our records show a certain level of consumption over a long period, several months in fact; we have checked our equipment and have not found any faults. After a sustained investigation, we are happy with the situation at Stone Beck Farm. Quite simply, they are paying for what they use.'

His comment was pretty final, I felt, and I began to wonder whether, over the months, the Chorleys had purchased lots of additional electrical apparatus, the result of which was a consumption much higher than hitherto. Certainly, John had his record player and an electric fire in his bedroom which he used as a kind of den. In the chill months of spring, autumn and winter, that would add substantially to the household electricity bill and, as I pondered the situation, I began to suspect that the Electricity Board was right. The Chorleys were paying for what they used – and yet, there was that nagging feeling about the meter's recording of consumption when everything was apparently switched off. Was this some kind of dodge the family was attempting, or was there a genuine reason? I felt sure that Janet Chorley was honest and sincere.

But the answer to the puzzle came the very next day in a most unexpected way; it came even before I'd had time to revisit Stone Beck Farm with the result of my chat to the Electricity Board's representative. Sergeant Blaketon rang me from his office in Ashfordly. 'Rhea, do you know some farmers called Chorley? Stone Beck Farm, Whemmelby?'

'Yes, I do, Sergeant.'

'And a son of theirs called John Frederick, seventeen years old, who works on that farm?'

'Yes, I know him too, Sergeant.'

'Well, I've been trying to ring them all afternoon. . . .'

'They'll be out, Sergeant; it's Brantsford Livestock Mart today, they'll be there. Why, is there something wrong?'

'Their son's been nicked, Rhea. He's in the cells at Eltering Police Station and his tractor and trailer have been confiscated, seized for evidence in fact. I want them to know and I want them to collect him, he's been granted bail. Their tractor'll have to stay until the drugs squad's finished examining it.'

'Arrested? His tractor and trailer seized? What's he done, Sergeant?'

'He's been growing cannabis, Rhea, tons of the stuff by all accounts. The Drugs Squad caught him with the stuff today; they'd got a bit of advance information from an informant and waited. He had a buyer waiting in one of the Eltering pubs. They've got him as well, he's a dealer. They've seized Chorley's tractor and trailer. He brought the stuff to sell in Eltering on the trailer, along with his tomato plants and cabbages. He does business with a local fruit and vegetable dealer.'

'He's a bit simple, Sergeant.' I felt I had to alert Blaketon to this fact. 'Not certifiable, but a bit light in the intellectual department.'

'He had to be simple to try to flog the stuff like that ... anyway, Rhea, the Drugs Squad is applying for a search warrant for Stone Beck Farm. They reckon that if the lad was producing such quantities, there'll be more on the farm.'

'So where's he growing it?' I asked. 'I was at the farm recently; I did a tour of the entire house and all the outbuildings and I never saw a leaf of cannabis. Are you sure he's growing it on the farm?'

'And why would you want to tour a farmhouse like that, Rhea?' he asked.

I explained my purpose, adding that I had not resolved the electrical problem for Mrs Chorley, when he commented, 'You'd know a cannabis plant if you saw one during your tour of that house, would you, Rhea? You'd not get it confused with a tomato or potato or something exotic from a hothouse?'

'No, I'd recognize cannabis,' I tried to assure him.

'Well, you'd better go along with the drugs wizards,' he told me. 'Young Chorley's pal has told him to say nothing so I've no idea where the stuff's grown. But there's usually plenty of available space around a farm. And I don't want the family warned in advance, Rhea! Otherwise they might destroy the lot!'

And so it was, later than evening, that I was driven to Stone Beck Farm at Whemmelby by a couple of Drugs Squad detectives.

My job was to inform the Chorleys of John's whereabouts and ask one of them to go and collect him from Eltering Police Station while the Drugs Squad officers searched the premises. I was also there to add a uniformed presence, just in case there was trouble. It was while thinking about this development that I realized why the Chorleys' electricity account was so high – quite clearly, young John had been cultivating his cannabis plants with heaters and lights. But where? Somehow, he must have established a connection with the mains cables. When we arrived and explained our presence, Jack Chorley was preparing for milking and he seemed unfazed by our appearance on his premises; Janet, on the other hand, was concerned for her son and she volunteered to drive to Eltering to collect him. Within a matter of moments, she was heading out of the gate in the Land-rover while Jack said, 'So what's all this about, Mr Rhea? I didn't quite catch on.'

'It's your lad,' I spoke in the language of the area. 'He's been arrested, Jack, for growing cannabis.'

'Cannabis? What's that? We only grow what we can sell hereabouts. Cabbages, kale, sugar beet and such stuff. Taties sometimes, and beans.'

One of the Drugs officers, Detective Sergeant Rogan, smiled at me as he said to Jack, 'This stuff's pretty saleable too, Mr Chorley, and on the right market it can fetch a good price, but it's illegal. Under the Dangerous Drugs Act of 1951, section 10, it is an offence to cultivate cannabis. We have evidence that your son has been growing illegal plants, Mr Chorley, cannabis in other words. And we've reason to believe he's been cultivating it here, on the farm.'

'Has he, by gum? Cannabis? I've never heard of the stuff! So where's he been growing it? I've noticed nowt different in our fields. Anyroad, why would he want to grow summat foreign? There's no call for foreign foods in these parts.'

I decided it was my turn to speak to this farmer. 'Mr Chorley,' I said slowly, 'one of the problems which is going to give the police and the public the biggest worries in the future is the illegal use of dangerous drugs.'

'I've heard all about that,' he agreed. 'Heroin, opium and such like.'

'Yes, well, cannabis is one of those drugs. It comes from a plant, Mr Chorley, and your lad, John, has been growing that plant.'

'He never has! The young sod!'

'What these officers want to know, Mr Chorley, is where John has been growing it. They've got a search warrant; they've got to find and then confiscate all John's plants, you see.'

'Well, they can look wherever they want. It's not anywhere in my fields, I can tell you that. Nor in my greenhouse. I've a few tomatoes there and a cucumber plant doing well, and other things like lettuces, but there's none of them foreign things.'

'So what other buildings have you?' asked Rogan. 'Is there a disused room or barn or something along similar lines that John might have used? It might even be some distance from the house.'

'Nay, lad, there's nowt like that. We make use of every bit of space; we can't afford empty spaces when money has to be made. I've even got gooseberry bushes growing in a patch behind the house, a patch you'd never think was big enough to grow daffodils on, and my missus keeps hens on a patch as big as your handkerchief. And they lay good eggs, brown 'uns. Waste not, want not, that's our motto.'

In an attempt to locate the illicit cannabis cultivation centre, I decided to refer to the exorbitant electricity bills, knowing the payments would eventually come from Jack's account.

'Jack, your missus has been complaining about high electricity bills, hasn't she? For a few months now.'

'Aye, she has, Mr Rhea.'

'So have you any idea where that power is being used? Can you see what I'm getting at? If your lad is cultivating exotic plants, he'll need heat and light, and a secure building somewhere.'

He pondered awhile and I could see his brain working slowly around to the idea that his son might be the cause of those high invoices.

'You mean our lad might be growing that stuff and making a fortune from it while we're paying his electric bills?' he muttered.

'Well, it's just a thought,' I shrugged, adding mischievously, 'It's one way of making a useful profit. But your Janet has been bothered about some very high bills in recent months and it does seem odd that they coincide with John's new cannabis business. It's a case of finding his hothouse.'

'The young sod!' he grunted. 'That lad's not as daft as I

thought he was. By gum, if you can get other folks to pay your expenses, you can allus make a big profit . . . now you mention it, Mr Rhea, I might just know where he's been growing that stuff.'

'Really?' I raised my eyebrows. 'And where might that be?'

'See our house?' He pointed to the handsome, well-proportioned building.

'Yes,' I nodded, and we all looked at the front of the house. As we viewed it, the domestic quarters were to the left of the long building, with accommodation for the cattle on the right, all under one long roof.

'It's what they call a long house, Mr Rhea. A traditionally built moorland farmhouse with the living part and cow-house all joined together in one long building. They did that in olden days, Mr Rhea, as a way of keeping the house warm in winter. The heat of the cattle in their shippen during wintertime helped to warm the living-quarters.'

'Right,' I nodded. 'I know that.'

'Well,' he said, 'the loft space above the cow-house isn't used these days – years ago, farm-hands slept there. They ate in the farmhouse and slept in the loft; they used a lot of candles, I'm told. It's quite separate from the house as the entrance is through the cow-house. Nowadays, there's nowt up there, we don't even use it as a hay loft. It's been empty for years; there's no windows, as you see.'

'But from here, it looks as if there's no useable space at all above your cow-house,' I said, looking at the frontal view of the house. 'I can see the stalls below and I'd say there's only the roof above.'

'Aye, well, that's where you're wrong, Mr Rhea. There is some space above them cowstalls, as big as if not bigger than a loft. Bags of room, but no light or windows.'

'So how does anyone get in there?' was my next question.

'Up through the far end of the cow-house,' he said. 'There's a ladder and a trap door. . . . There used to be a way in from the house, years ago, but we had it bricked up.'

'Come on,' I said to everyone. Now, I realized why I had not found this place when examining the house for electrical supplies. From the domestic quarters, there was no entrance to the loft above the cow byre and it was easy for anyone, even the Electricity Board officials, to assume any power or light in that loft would be linked to the business power source. Clearly, it wasn't.

Before young John returned, his father led us up the wooden stairs and into the loft where we found an immense hoard of well-tended cannabis plants, all in small seed boxes and all being warmed and illuminated by a series of powerful lights and electric heaters linked to the domestic supply. It was like stepping into a hot house but because the loft had not been used for years, those sockets and plugs had been forgotten. Now, young John was making good use of them.

'Well, I'll be damned!' grunted his father. 'Who'd have thought this?'

Detective Sergeant Rogan then formally asked him, 'Mr Chorley, did you know about this crop?'

'Nay, lad, I'd no idea. But what a grand spot for growing things. . . .'

To cut short a long story, young John was put on probation for the unauthorized intentional cultivation of cannabis; his simple-mindedness went in his favour and the court accepted he had no idea of what the plant really was. It was also accepted that his parents had no knowledge of the crop he was cultivating.

The man he supplied, and who, it transpired, had persuaded John to grow the plants, won a sentence of three years for various drugs offences. As for John, his entire stock of cannabis plants was confiscated: although the tractor and trailer were restored to the farm. Afterwards, his father decided that, with some modifications, the loft would be ideal for raising a variety of commercially viable plants.

'If it hadn't been for our John,' he smiled. 'I'd never have known about that spot . . . it had gone clean out of my mind. It had never been used for years. But I believe in using every bit of space, Mr Rhea, for profit that is. So now it's going to earn its keep – I'll put some roof windows in and it's already got power and light fitted. Good thinking years ago by somebody, that was.'

But Janet Chorley was more down to earth. When I called some weeks after the court case, she said, 'You know what, Mr Rhea. Our John made a real profit out of yon drug plant he was growing. He's got a useful savings account now, I thought the court would have done summat about that, confiscated it mebbe.'

'The court wouldn't be able to touch his money,' I said. 'There was no proof his savings were directly associated with the cultivation of drugs.'

'Mebbe not, but he put pounds and pounds into his bank account, saving up for a car, he said. But you know what made me very cross?'

'No?' She had never mentioned the illegality of her son's enterprise and so I was awaiting her reaction to this type of law-breaking.

'He paid nowt in business expenses!' she grumbled. 'And here was me, slaving away with my hens and eggs and taties and turnips, all to pay our 'lectric bills, and all the time he's selling his stuff for a big profit – and never paying me a penny!'

'Well, it's all over now,' I tried to sympathize with her. 'He knows he mustn't grow the stuff and his dad's going to use the old loft for something else. If he wants to make himself some money without breaking the law, John will have to stick to hens and pigs and things normally reared on a farm, I reckon. And if he likes gardening, he can grow plants and sell them to dealers.'

'He'll have to buy his seeds and boxes first!' she snapped. 'I'm not letting him have anything from my stock! He'll have to go to market and buy his own. He has to learn, hasn't he, Mr Rhea? Besides, he won't have much money for a while, will he?'

'Won't he?' I said. 'I thought he'd made quite a profit from his gardening!'

'Aye, mebbe so,' she laughed. 'But he owes me a fair bit for his 'lectric bills. I haven't worked it out yet but it goes back a few months! Once he's paid all that off, he can start thinking about spending money on starting another business. But not until!'

As I left the farm, I realized John's parental punishment was as good as any fine the court might have imposed. His mother would make sure he paid for his mistake! But I must admit his crop had produced some very fine plants of the genus *Cannabis*. I wondered if, with a reduced profit margin, he would produce such splendid tomatoes and cucumbers.

Just as the naïve John Chorley had, at the outset, no idea he was committing a criminal offence by cultivating cannabis, neither did Abraham Smithers regard his activities as illegal.

Abraham and his wife, Polly, lived in the Old School House at Milthorpe. Years ago, this fine stone building had been a remote but thriving village primary school, but, in time, numbers of pupils had dwindled and the school had closed. Following its closure, any pupils from Milthorpe were taken into Aidensfield by bus where they joined classes at Aidensfield primary school. Senior children were taken on to Ashfordly Secondary Modern or Strensford Grammar School.

Abraham and Polly, both in their early forties and lecturers in environmental studies at a polytechnic on Teesside, had fallen in love with the notion of living a rustic life in the middle of the heathery heights of the North York Moors and had bought the old school. After much expense and hard work they converted it into an impressive dwelling house, and the former playground became a garden renowned for its flowers. Of particular interest was Abraham's annual and highly colourful display of splendid dahlias which flourished in the autumn.

The Smithers had no children, but they did have a small red Ford Anglia van which they used to travel across the moors to their work on Teesside, and it was also used to carry their flowers to shows and exhibitions. The nature of their lecturing work meant they were frequently at home to cultivate their little spread of England, Polly giving valued support to Abraham in his efforts. There is no doubt that Abraham was an authority on dahlias, showing them and lecturing about them both locally and nationally, and contributing specialist articles to gardening magazines and newspapers. That he was an expert on the flower was never in doubt, and to anyone who either listened to him or saw him at work in his garden, he was clearly devoted to these gorgeous blooms.

The snag was they were also enjoyed by moorland sheep.

It was a long time before I became aware of Abraham's never-ending battle against the invading sheep, but the first intimation came in the form of a complaint from Hannah Winspear. Hannah, a dour, unmarried lady in her late sixties, owned a flock of black-faced sheep which she kept on the open moorland above and behind Milthorpe. Hannah, who lived alone in a small stone cottage on the edge of the moors, was a familiar sight in her old navy-blue gaberdine mackintosh, black wellington boots and battered grey trilby hat; she always carried a shepherd's crook which sometimes served as a tall walking stick.

Her flock was about eighty in number and her animals were identified by a splash of blue marker on the fleece of their left shoulders.

To help her tend the sheep, she relied on a black and white border collie called Lassie, and from time to time she and Lassie would drive some of the animals into Ashfordly livestock mart, invariably blocking the lanes with the animals along the five-mile route. At market, she might buy further animals for her own flock, or she would breed her own lambs in the spring. In and around the district, therefore, Hannah was a regular sight and a much-loved character. Then one morning, she rang me from the telephone kiosk in Milthorpe.

'Is that Mr Rhea?' she shouted into the mouthpiece.

'Speaking,' I answered, instantly recognizing her voice.

'Somebody's stealing my ewes,' she hollered. 'You'd better come and see me and I'll tell you all about it.'

'How about eleven o'clock this morning?' I suggested.

'Right,' she bellowed, slamming down the receiver. Although Hannah had a soft and rather pleasant speaking voice, she always shouted down a telephone. The shopkeepers she rang on a regular basis always reckoned she didn't need a telephone; she could shout her orders from her house, but it didn't work like that. When facing anyone, her voice was quiet and calm; it was only the telephone which seemed to compel her to bellow. At eleven, as agreed, I arrived at Hob Hole House, her small, idyllic smallholding and home, and found her outside, sweeping elderberry leaves from the yard. A dozen hens and bantams clucked at my approach and a couple of ginger cats emerged from the house to gaze at me.

But with the coming of autumn, the leaves were falling and the solitary tree beside her house was managing to produce an inordinate amount of fallen foliage. I stood for a few moments to admire the stunning views across the moors and dales and to think that such a place would appeal to any townie – at least for the summer. In the winter, it would be a different story with drifting snow, gales and numbing cold. A long hard winter always sorts out the genuine country lovers from the wannabees. But Hannah had always lived here, even as a child, and knew no other home.

'Now then Mr Rhea.' She leant her brush against the wall of the house and said, 'You'd better come in, I've got the kettle on.'

The house was sparsely furnished, the kitchen also serving as her lounge, and a blazing log fire burnt in the Yorkist range. The floor comprised stone flags covered with home-made clip rugs, and the brasses around the fireplace gleamed in the light. A blackened kettle was suspended over the heat and was singing happily, puffing steam from its spout and lid, as she found a teapot and heaped in some tea-leaves.

'You'll have a mug of tea and a scone, Mr Rhea?'

'Thanks, Hannah, that'll be fine.'

As I sat at her simple wooden table, I opened the proceedings by asking, 'So what's this about somebody stealing your sheep?'

'Well, you know how they behave, Mr Rhea, my sheep, I mean. In the daytime, they're on the moor tops and at night, they wander down into the village and sleep on the green. They've allus done that, year in and year out. They keep the grass and verges trimmed. That's why Milthorpe is always so tidy.'

'That's right, I know that,' I acknowledged.

'And when there's bad weather about, they'll come down from the moors even in the daytime – it's allus a sign of bad weather when the sheep come down from the moors out of their usual time.'

'Yes, I know that. They're very good weather forecasters,' I smiled.

'So at this time of year,' she continued in her droll manner, 'they're down here quite a lot, munching grass around the green and things.'

'Right,' I nodded.

'And if the weather's going to be fine and dry, they'll wander back up to their heeafts on the moors.'

'Got it,' I nodded again, knowing that a heeaft is the local name for a sheep's home patch of moorland. The sheep become accustomed to a particular part of the moor and will always return there if they leave; the word heeaft means home.

'Well, Mr Rhea, some of 'em aren't getting back to their heeafts.'

'You've done a count, have you?' I asked her.

'I have that!' she affirmed. 'A month back, I did a count on the moors, me and Lassie that is, and we had seventy-nine ewes. Next time I counted 'em, there was one missing. Now t'same thing happened last week – another one missing. And again this morning. Yesterday, Mr Rhea, I did a check on the moors. Seventy-seven last night and only seventy-six this morning. One's going missing each time, Mr Rhea. Three gone. As sure as shot.'

'And all have got your blue mark on the left shoulder?'

'Aye, they have. I've asked my neighbours if my ewes have strayed onto their land, but they say not. And they're not lying dead, I don't think we've had foxes up there, Mr Rhea.'

'Could you have made a mistake while counting?' I didn't like to suggest she might have made an error, but it was a question I had to ask – Sergeant Blaketon would surely ask me the same thing.

'Nay, lad, not me. I've been counting my sheep for years, I

know how to count 'em properly. What's been happening, Mr Rhea, is that the whole flock comes down to the village green some nights, and one less goes back next morning.'

'But it's not happening on a regular basis?' I said.

'Not every day, no. It's every now and again,' she agreed. 'It might have been happening for quite some time, Mr Rhea, because some weeks back I noticed I was short of a sheep or two. I thought we'd mebbe had rustlers at night, but this is getting too regular to be accidents or lost sheep dying out there.'

'So which days are we talking about? Can you remember?'

'Monday morning last week, one had gone. Again on Thursday last week. And this morning.'

'Today's Monday. That makes it a second Monday,' I said, thinking there might be some kind of routine to these thefts. 'I wonder if the coming Thursday might be another busy day for your thief?'

'I can keep my eyes open, Mr Rhea. They're vanishing in the village, so somebody local's stealing them. There's no doubt about that.'

'Any idea who it might be?' was my next question.

'No, that's the trouble. I haven't. If I had, I'd go and have words; they're depriving me of my income, Mr Rhea.'

'It won't be easy, laying a trap for the thief or keeping watch if it's not happening on a regular basis.'

'I know that. I've tried keeping watch myself, but I've never seen anything. But I have to report these thefts to you, for insurance purposes.'

'I'll record it in our crime reports,' I assured her. 'And I will pass word to our patrols so they're all aware of it, and, of course, I'll keep my own eyes open. I'll do my best to be around on Thursday morning, just in case.'

'Me too,' she said.

'We'd better not be seen together while we keep watch – two sets of eyes in two different places will be more beneficial. What time do you think they're being taken?'

'It's hard to say, Mr Rhea. I usually check 'em around half-eight or nine o'clock, they've been gone by then.'

'Right, leave it with me, Hannah. I'll see what transpires on Thursday. Let's hope we can catch the culprit.'

'Thanks, Mr Rhea.'

'In the meantime, give me a call if any more vanish,' I said. 'And the sooner I'm told about a loss the better. If we can catch the culprit in possession of the animal, it means we've a good case to put before the court.'

The trouble with sheep stealing is that most thieves kill the animals and strip away their fleeces immediately, even before transporting them from the scene; this removes any identifying marks and thus it is difficult, if not impossible, to prove that the carcass in their possession has been stolen. If someone was stealing Hannah's ewes, then I was sure they'd be using that technique. It would be a very difficult task to catch the thief, prove the source of their carcasses and then secure a conviction – but I would try. I was slightly unsure that these disappearances were thefts – in spite of their amazing homing instincts, moorland sheep can go astray. They are not fenced in and are free to roam over a huge area of land on the moors and in the surrounding villages. Sometimes, they can get trapped in ditches or among barbed wire and sometimes, they can die from poison or disease without their owners realizing until some time later. And, of course, many get killed by motor vehicles on the moorland roads, the sheep's road sense being comparable to that of some weekend drivers.

Bearing in mind these possibilities, I had to bow to Hannah's superior knowledge of her flock. If she felt some of her animals were being stolen, then I felt she was right. As I departed from her delightful house, I made a mental note to patrol Milthorpe next Thursday morning. I would have to inform Sergeant Blaketon too, so that my duties could accommodate this period of observations.

When I telephoned him, he said, 'If you think those sheep are being stolen, Rhea, then you are perfectly entitled to keep observations for the thief. But if my experience is anything to go by, those missing ewes will have been knocked down by a passing lorry or wandered off or got trapped somewhere.'

'That's possible, Sergeant,' I agreed. 'But I tend to side with Hannah in thinking they've been stolen.'

'There've been no other local reports of sheep stealing and I doubt if a thief would find it profitable to take just one sheep every once in a while. They like a vanful to make it economic. But yes, you might be right, so keep observations and if you catch the villain, call me.'

On the Wednesday of that week, by one of those odd coincidences that life tends to throw up from time to time, I had to call on Roy Hamilton who farmed at Lee Ridge Farm, Fieldholme, a small moorland village on the northern extremity of my beat. Roy's firearm certificate was due for renewal and I decided to conduct my quarterly check of his stock register at the same time. I rang in advance to make sure he would be on the premises and we settled on 2 p.m. as the time for my visit.

Roy was a decent young man who had rented this farm from Fieldholme Estate; in his late thirties, married with two sons and a daughter, all at primary school, he was a hard worker who managed to extract a decent living from his sparse patch of moorland. In this, he was helped by his wife, Jill, who worked part-time in an Ashfordly haberdashery shop. Like most of the hill farmers of these moors, he kept sheep which roamed freely on the heathery heights above his farm, and also maintained a small dairy herd which grazed in the dale below his farm.

After completing my business over the inevitable mug of tea, scone and piece of apple pie, I rose to leave when he said, 'While you're here, Mr Rhea, I've something I ought mebbe to mention to you.'

'Yes?' I folded my notebook and slipped my pen back into my pocket.

'Well, it's a bit funny, but in the last few days, I've had three stray sheep turn up on my land.'

'Live ones?' I asked.

'Oh yes, very healthy ones. Black-faces.'

'And their markings?' I asked.

'Blue flashes on the left shoulder,' Roy told me. 'All of them.'

'Do you know Hannah Winspear?' I asked. 'From Milthorpe?'

He shook his head. 'No, sorry, it's a fair way from here, Mr Rhea. Can't say I know the lady.'

'Well, in the last few days she's lost three black-face ewes, mebbe more. They've disappeared from her flock during the morning, she reckons, over a few days.'

'These aren't mine and there's nobody in our part of the world has a blue flash on the shoulder, Mr Rhea. I thought about advertising I'd found them, but if they're your friend Hannah's, she'd better come and look at them, and take them back.'

'I'll get her to come over to see you,' I promised. 'But how did they get here? It must be miles from Milthorpe!'

'And there's a river in between,' he reminded me. 'Sheep wouldn't wander that far and they wouldn't cross the river, not all three of them at different times.'

'So they've been brought here?'

'Aye, I think so. We think somebody's dumped them on our land.'

'We?'

'Well, my wife. Jill, that is. She was on the way to work the other morning and spotted a red van. It was parked on the moors on the edge of my land. There was a sheep near it, she said; at first, she thought it was somebody in the act of stealing one of our sheep, then she saw a chap shoo the sheep away . . . it had a blue mark on its shoulder. By the time Jill got there, the van had gone and she couldn't get its number. And the more Jill thought about it, the more she thought the sheep had been dumped from the van. And that would account for the others, wouldn't it? Somebody dumping them on our land, for some odd reason.'

'Is Jill in now?' I asked.

'No, she's at work.'

'And the sheep? Are they fit and well? Not diseased or sick or injured?'

'No, not at all. They're all in good condition. I've got them in a pen now, Mr Rhea, I decided to isolate them from my own flock, to be on the safe side, just in case they do have a disease which would infect mine.'

'Right, I'll get Hannah to come across and look at them. Thanks for telling me. Now, if you or Jill see that red van again, can you note its number? I'd like to know what the driver's up to!'

'And so would I!' grinned Roy.

It was while returning home, on a glorious drive across the moors, that I recollected the red van which was owned by Abraham and Polly Smithers. I'd often seen it chugging across these moors because this was on the route from Milthorpe to Teesside. It was quite a distinctive vehicle and the only red van within a large radius. If Abraham and Polly were removing Hannah's sheep, why would they dump them on Roy's patch of moorland? There was only one way to find out.

Accordingly, I popped into Milthorpe and found them both in their garden, tending the dahlias in the former playground. And the little red van was parked outside the house. I entered the garden and admired the flowers, with Abraham, a strange character with long, straggly hair and an equally long straggly beard, explaining to me the different characteristics of his dahlias.

Eventually I found the opportune moment to refer to the reason for my visit. 'You drive from here some mornings, don't you? To Teesside?'

'I do indeed, Mr Rhea, and a glorious run it is too. One gets very poetic feelings, enjoying those moors at dawn.'

'Have you ever given a sheep a lift?' I asked, partly in mirth and partly with serious intent.

'Indeed I have, Mr Rhea, on more than one occasion, I might add. The confounded things come down from the moors and jump over the walls into my garden. I have lost scores of flowers due to rampaging sheep, Mr Rhea, and although I do not like to be unkind to animals, I do feel they should remain where they belong, and that's on the moors.'

'Really?'

'Yes, indeed. On most occasions when I discover them, they

run away and jump back over the walls to escape, but from time to time, I manage to corner one or two. I seize them by the horns and manhandle them into my van. Then, on my way to work, I return them from whence they came: the moors.'

'Those sheep, the ones which invade your garden, do not live on the part of the moors where you dumped them, Abraham. Sheep are not wild animals, they are owned by local people and they have their own patch of moorland. . . .'

'Are you suggesting I am being cruel to them?' he put to me. 'That is most certainly not my intention. I am an animal lover, Mr Rhea.'

'I'm sure you are. But I am saying you could be charged with larceny. Stealing sheep is a crime under section three of the Larceny Act of 1916.'

'Stealing them? I am not stealing them, Mr Rhea. I am simply removing them from my garden to safeguard my dahlias by returning them to their natural habitat.'

'The law might say you are permanently depriving their owners of the animals,' I countered. 'By taking them so far from their natural habitat, with a river preventing their return even if they could find their way, it might be said you were deliberately and permanently depriving the owners of their livestock.'

'But those things are semi-wild, Mr Rhea. . . .'

'I think that you, as a lecturer on the environment, should acquaint yourself with practicalities of living in the countryside, Abraham; you rely too much on theories instead of practicalities. Those sheep, you will note, the ones you have removed, have blue flashes on their shoulders. . . .'

'Through rubbing against some wet paint, I guess.'

'Through having blue dye spread on a particular place to indicate ownership, Abraham. The sheep you removed from their natural home belong to Hannah Winspear of Hob Hole House. The blue mark is hers. They have now been found and kept by a farmer at Fieldholme; he is called Roy Hamilton and he lives at Lee Ridge Farm. Because they might be diseased, Roy has had to segregate them from his own flock, all of which costs time and money.'

'Have I made a bit of a fool of myself? Shown my townie ignorance?'

'I rather think you have. Now, the next problem will be persuading my sergeant that you had no criminal intention when you took the animals. I think, first, a word with Hannah and an apology would be a good idea.'

'By me, you mean?'

'Yes. If you explain to her what you were doing and the thinking behind your actions, and perhaps with an offer to bring the animals back for her, then she might persuade us not to proceed with a charge of larceny. Or three charges of larceny to be precise, one for each animal.'

'Yes, Mr Rhea, I will do that. But, really, my dahlias are so important and the sheep manage to leap the walls. . . .'

'Perhaps you might invest in a high wire fence, Abraham? One that neither sheep nor deer can leap over.'

'Deer?'

'There are wild deer in our woods, Abraham, and they do love juicy fresh flowers. . . .'

'It was vandals in Middlesbrough,' he said.

'Here, it's wildlife that's the problem,' I smiled. 'But off you go. I will await developments with interest.'

Abraham did visit Hannah to apologize with a huge bunch of dahlias and she forgave him because he offered to bring back her missing sheep. Roy Hamilton was delighted too – his wife also got a bunch of dahlias and Abraham learned something about living in the environment about which he taught. And he bought some rolls of wire netting which he placed around his garden.

Sergeant Blaketon decided there was no criminal intent in this case and so the charge of sheep stealing did not proceed. 'Once, you could be hanged for stealing sheep,' he reminded me. 'That Abraham Smithers is a lucky man.'

'The sheep are lucky too,' I said. 'They survived their trial by ordeal.'

8

I must show out a flag and sign of love . . .
William Shakespeare (1564–1616)

Young men in love may be tempted to display all manner of signs to the lady of their passion. Some such indications might be very subtle and endearing, but others can be rather too intrusive and even embarrassing. Publicizing the name of one's heart's desire by sky-writing from an aeroplane or placing an advertisement in the newspapers are just two examples of the latter, but the purpose of such displays, in whatever form they take, is usually to impress a lady or to draw attention to the strength, skills, daring and desirability of the man in question.

Down the ages, young men have produced a wonderful variety of exhibitions which have been intended to impress the opposite sex or at the very least to make the lady of their dreams aware of their yearning existence. Such masculine efforts have included everything from the way they dress to the way they strive to win at sport; some will resort to impressive cars: others will behave in a bewildering range of outrageous ways and the more volatile will fight others in their desire to impress the female of the species.

It might be argued that town and city lads are more streetwise and more confident in the company of girls than rural youths: certainly, a lot of shy rural lads have found difficulty in striking up loving relationships with young women.

Even as I write these notes in 1997, the hills and moors around me are replete with unmarried country lads of all ages, bachelors for eternity. Such lads are tough, hard-working men with all the sexual desires of a healthy male; they are not homosexuals. It's just that they have not got around to finding a girlfriend and getting married. For these shy and uncultured youths, such a step would be a major event in their lives, something on the same unlikely level as piloting a space ship to the moon or becoming prime minister.

The Yorkshire Dales and North York Moors are rich with examples of clumsy attempts at courtship by rural lads. One story tells of a farm-lad who went out with the same girl for nineteen years. Eventually, as both reached the age of forty, the patient and long-suffering woman plucked up courage and asked, 'John, isn't it time we got married?' His response was, 'Yes, but who'd have us now?'

In another case, a farmer and his wife were concerned about their 22-year-old son, Dan. Throughout his teenage years and into young manhood, Dan had shown no interest in girls and then, one evening, much to their surprise and pleasure, he got shaved, put on his best suit complete with a tie, plastered his hair with water from the tap and said he was going out.

Dad, puzzled by this sudden and rather uncharacteristic behaviour asked, 'Where are you going, Dan?'

'I'm going out,' replied Dan, with just an air of mystery.

'Out?' asked his mother. 'Where to?'

There was a long pause before Dan answered most coyly, 'Down to the village. I'm going to see Mary Jane.'

'Mary Jane from Pasture House Farm?' beamed his father.

'Aye,' said the lad, rushing out of the house as he blushed crimson.

The parents were delighted. Mary Jane was a lovely young woman from a good family with a wide experience of farming. It would be a perfect match. In the hope this would develop into something of a serious and long-term nature, the parents decided to await their son's return, however late it might be. Sitting by their fireside on the lonely farm, they happily discussed the possible outcome of Dan's date, thinking their farm would soon have a woman in residence. There might even be children to continue the family links with the business, then

Mum and Dad might then be able to retire. There is no doubt it was a very happy and hopeful evening for them. Then, around eleven o'clock, they heard the back door open and in came Dan. He hung his cap on the hook inside the door, and then entered the living-room. Mum and Dad waited expectantly for some kind of report about the evening.

When nothing appeared to be forthcoming, Dad asked, 'Well, Dan, did you see Mary Jane?'

'Aye,' said Dan, his eyes gleaming with happiness. 'And if I hadn't ducked down behind that wall, she might have seen me.'

Perhaps it is the isolated nature and long hours of a farm-lad's work that nurtures this shyness and prevents him meeting available girls; I know one moorland farm which boasts seven sons, only one of whom has married. The men's parents, each in their eighties, continue to live on the premises from where they direct operations, and so the lads perform all the domestic and administrative work as well as undertaking all the tough work on the farm. Quite simply, their long hours and isolated home life have kept them away from suitable young women.

In my work as a village constable on a large rural beat, I came across such circumstances on a surprisingly regular basis. I must admit there were times I felt sorry for the lads in question – quite simply, their only relaxation was sleep. Farm work was so enduring and demanding that time-off was never considered; consequently, many of these isolated lads had no opportunity to meet other youngsters, except perhaps at a cattle market or agricultural show. Even those outings were associated with their work. That being so, I wondered how any of them ever managed to strike up a relationship with a desirable young woman. Some did manage it, of course, and got married to live happily ever after, but many did not.

It was an event at Briggsby which provided me with just one example of a farm-lad's determination to create an initiative for love. Having undertaken a brief foot patrol of that village, I was driving back to Aidensfield on a beautiful sunny and clear September morning. As I descended the long, steep hill from the lofty elevation upon which Briggsby is situated, I had a clear view of the patchwork of dry-stone walls and multi-coloured open fields which were spread before me at the far side of the dale. I began to admire the colours and patterns of that scene, the recently ploughed cornfields in deep brown, the patch of green sugar beet, the softer green meadows and yellowed grazing lands, all of which were separated one from the other by centuries-old dry-stone walls.

Built without mortar, these amazing structures have survived in spite of the weather and the wildlife which lives within the gaps among the stones. Although farmers of this region tend to graze their sheep on the open moors, some flocks are maintained in fields and meadows and it was while admiring that long-distance view that I noticed a peculiarity among some sheep which were grazing in one of those enclosed fields. Although, from my vantage point, the animals were little more than off-white dots on the distant landscape, I realized that some were spelling out a word.

In capital letters, the word read SUE. As I was driving at the time and concentrating upon my actions, I must admit I did not immediately realize what I was seeing. Initially, I regarded it as merely a gathering of sheep on a distant hillside which happened to have formed themselves into what appeared to be a word. I realized that I might be imagining that word, that I might have seen the animals create a recognizable design that no one else would have noticed, particularly in those circumstances.

I drove on, marvelling at the coincidence before me, but not paying any further attention. Later, I thought it was one of those natural phenomena which sometimes occur, like cloud formations which look like human faces or clumps of distant shrubs which grow in such a way that they assume the shape of animals. Different people may see different shapes in these circumstances. Three or four days later, however, the sheep were spelling the same name but a week later, the word had changed. Now it was SUE XX.

I had now come to realize, of course, that sheep cannot spell like that, nor could they be expected to form themselves into these very clear messages on such a regular basis. Obviously, someone was persuading them to stand together in such a way that these messages could be read from the distant road. I began to wonder how it was achieved. Sheep are not regarded as the most intelligent of animals and I did not think any shepherd or farmer, however skilled, could persuade them to stand in that formation for what amounted to a considerable time. Formation dancing and dressage among sheep was unknown at that time.

As the days went by, the messages became even more intriguing through the use of more sheep or by making smaller letters – one day, the sheep said I LOVE SUE, and on another occasion the message was SUE X IAN. By this stage, I had realized the field in question belonged to Longrigg Farm, the home of the Sedman family. And they had a son called Ian who worked on the farm. I had come across Ian from time to time, recalling that he was a shy lad in his late teens or early twenties who rarely left the premises. Whenever he did leave, it was usually on his racing pedal cycle which he rode into Ashfordly or Aidensfield to buy something personal like a new LP or pair of shoes. I'd never seen him in any of the local pubs, nor had I noticed him attending any of the village dances. He appeared to lead a very lonely and isolated life.

Although I regularly called at the farm during my duties, I had no intention of embarrassing Ian in front of his family by referring to his messages of love, even if they had been presented in such a way that the whole world could read them.

I considered Ian to be just another of a long list of farm labourers who seemed destined to the life of a bachelor. But while thinking of Ian in these circumstances, it was inevitable that I wondered about the identity of the mysterious Sue.

And then one morning, as I was performing an early patrol in my Mini-van, I found myself descending that hill out of Briggsby and, walking ahead of me on the road, was Ian Sedman. On this occasion, the sheep were not displaying any message. Ian, however, was heading the same direction as I, so I stopped and asked if he wanted a lift.

'Aye, thanks, Mr Rhea,' he said, as he climbed into the passenger seat of my police van.

'Where are you heading?' I asked.

'Aidensfield,' he told me. 'The surgery, for these bandages to be changed. I can't grip my handlebars, otherwise I'd have biked in.'

He held up his left hand which was swathed in bandages and when I asked him what had happened, he told me he'd sliced the palm of his hand with a turnip cutter causing a very deep wound. He had to attend the surgery once a week for the wound to be examined and to get the dressings changed. He was walking to the surgery because his parents were busy with some new calves.

'The doctor reckons there'll be no lasting damage,' he said with some relief. 'I didn't cut through any nerves or owt like that. I could be using my hand by this time next week.'

As the journey would take only six or seven minutes and we were alone in the van, I decided to ask about the sheep. I wanted to know how he'd persuaded them to stand in formation – and I might just learn a little about the mysterious Sue.

'I saw those messages of yours,' I smiled at him. 'Nice work, Ian.'

He blushed crimson but said nothing; I wondered if he'd realized that everyone passing along the road would be able to read them. Most of the local people would realize he was their creator.

'How did you persuade those sheep to make the letters?' I continued, seeing that he was embarrassed about the matter.

'It was an accident at first, Mr Rhea. I put some feed down and thought I'd spell Sue's name on the ground. I mean, nobody would have seen it. Then the sheep came and started to eat the stuff and next thing I knew Sue's name was spelt in sheep on our hillside. That feed's a concentrate. From sacks . . . you just walk along and pour it out. It's dead easy to make patterns and letters with it, Mr Rhea.'

'So having done it once, you thought you'd do it again?'

'Yes, it was fun, making up different messages and then

seeing if the sheep would make the letters.'

'Clever stuff,' I praised him. 'So what's Sue think to it all?'

'She's never said.' He blushed even deeper. 'I don't know whether she's seen them or not . . . it was just a bit of fun, you know. Nowt serious. I got kind of carried away with it.'

'I like the idea.' I realized I had not to make fun of this behaviour. 'And I bet Sue did as well!'

'You really think so?' There was a spark of interest here, encouragement almost.

'You could always ask her,' was my next suggestion.

'Nay, I'm too shy to do that,' he said. 'I mean, it's not as if I actually came up with the idea of the sheep. . . .'

'But you did spell her name out in their feed, didn't you? If you can come up with ideas like that, I'll bet Sue would be keen to know how those letters were made by the sheep,' I told him. 'It's better than spelling her name across a field with turnips!'

'My dad thought it was a daft idea,' he said, with his head down.

'That's because he never thought of it!' I laughed. 'Anyway, you've done it now and it might get you talking to Sue one of these days. . . .'

'She lives in Briggsby. I sometimes bike over there but I've never seen her knocking about the place. She comes down that hill on her bike every day to work, though,' he told me with some excitement in his voice. 'That's why I put the messages in that field, so she could see them.'

'But you don't know whether she has seen them or not?'

'No, no idea,' he admitted.

'Well, you'll just have to wait until she says something, or you'll have to pluck up the courage to ask her, won't you? You'll have to keep riding over to Briggsby in the hope you'll bump into her somewhere.'

'I'm not very good with girls, I never know what to say. . . .'

'The trick is to get them to talk about themselves,' I suggested, but I did wonder whether he would ever pluck up the courage to break the proverbial ice with Sue. Even though she came from Briggsby, a tiny hill-top community, I did not know who Sue was and decided not to press him on what was quite a delicate and personal matter. Nonetheless, I felt I had given him a slice of encouragement and some useful advice. Very soon we were approaching Aidensfield and I said I would take him right to the surgery; I had to pass it on my way home so it was not out of my way. As we eased to a halt outside, I noticed a slender, young, dark-haired woman with a bicycle. She had just dismounted and was placing the bike against the surgery wall.

She would be about eighteen, I thought, and I realized it was the young woman I'd sometimes seen cycling from Briggsby to Aidensfield around 8.30 on a weekday morning. I brought the van to a halt only feet away from her and as I waited for Ian to climb out of my vehicle, I saw him blushing crimson.

'Is that Sue?' I asked him, guessing the answer from his demeanour.

'Aye, she works here, she's the new receptionist,' he said.

'Then this is your big chance, Ian,' I told him. 'Out you get – your new life starts at this very minute!'

'Nay, Mr Rhea, I can't . . . I mean, I can't start talking to her, can I? I mean, she doesn't know me.'

'When you report your arrival for the surgery, she'll know who you are, and if she's a local girl. . . .'

'She is, she lives at Briggsby, like I said. I often go there on my bike, for a ride round, you know, of an evening, in case she's out and about.'

'Well, if she lives at Briggsby and cycles to work at Aidensfield, she'll have seen those messages, Ian, she couldn't miss them. . . .'

'By, I feel daft now,' he muttered. 'Doing a trick like that. . . .'

As we were chatting, Sue disappeared into the building to prepare for the day's morning surgery and for the arrival of Dr Williams. I could see that Ian was debating whether or not he should follow her inside. But his mind was made up with the arrival of Dr Williams in his Rover.

'Morning, Ian. First in the queue again, eh?' he said, as he emerged from the car. 'Give me time to get myself organized and then come in. Sue will see to you and get your file out.'

'It's time to go,' I said. 'And good luck!'

Ian was blushing furiously as he left me and made for the surgery entrance, so I tooted my horn as I drove away. I did not know Sue personally; clearly, she was a local girl who was settling down to her new job and I felt sure she would welcome some attention from the shy Ian.

It was two weeks later, on a Saturday, when I saw two youngsters, a girl and a youth, riding their bikes together along the lane towards Maddleskirk. As I passed, I realized they were Ian and Sue.

I tooted the horn of mv van, but they did not respond. They were too engrossed in one another to notice the passing of a village constable.

And I never noticed any more sheep spelling love messages in the hills.

Ian Sedman's method of proclaiming his love through choreographed sheep was quite harmless and rather charming. To this could be added a whole range of similar love messages, like the youth who named his prize sow after his girlfriend, another who used a muck-spreader to splatter his girlfriend's name in manure across the runway of a disused airfield and yet another who wrote his girlfriend's name in white paint across the green tarpaulin which covered a haystack.

While such pranks were of little professional interest to the local constabulary, the area around Aidensfield later suffered a different type of rural message. At first, no one knew whether this latest outbreak of creating messages in the earth was done out of spite, anger, revenge or even whether it was a form of twisted love, but on that occasion it was very much a matter for the police.

Someone had ploughed up part of the cricket pitch at Thackerston. It happened in the early weeks of the cricket season and the vandalism occurred during the night of a Tuesday/Wednesday. At first, no one was quite sure of the purpose of the long, curved but rather shallow furrow which had been cut from the pristine turf. It extended right across the pitch midway between the wickets, but it was the chance remark of a sheep farmer on the hills above who told the captain the mark was a giant letter J without the crosspiece.

From his vantage point, he could see the entire cut. It began at one side of the pitch, about ten yards from the middle of it, crossed the pitch at right angles to a point about ten yards on the other side, and then terminated in a curve which formed the hook of the J.

It was some twenty-five yards long but the cut itself was quite narrow. I was called just after nine on the Wednesday morning and went to inspect it with the volunteer groundsman, Harry Wheater. He was a 45-year-old plumber who lived in Thackerston. A tall, rather gangly man with rounded specs, overalls and little hair, he was a keen cricketer and willing worker for many village organizations.

'So what's caused that furrow?' I put to him.

'It's too small for a plough,' he suggested. 'I think it's been done with a rotavator, Nick, quite a powerful one judging by the fact it's gone through the turf.'

'They don't have lights fitted, do they?' I commented.

'Not as a rule, Nick. No. Why?'

'Well, it would mean the damage was done in the darkness. I'm wondering how much the rotavator driver would be able to see ahead of himself or around him.'

'Not a great lot, I'd say. He might have had to operate with a hand torch. That wouldn't give him much of a headlight, not like tractor lights would have done.'

'I'm wondering, Harry, whether this damage was done with some plan or skill, or whether it was a random attack on the pitch, literally ploughing in the dark. Do you think the cut was deliberately made across the wicket rather than along it, or did the perpetrator simply bring the machine here and let it rip without any real plan?'

'He has managed to make a letter J,' said Harry, thoughtfully.

'Or,' I said, 'he might have brought the machine here in a van or something and left the headlights burning; that would give him a good view of the pitch.'

'He'd need to keep his engine running if he did that, otherwise he'd soon flatten his battery. Blazing headlights can flatten a battery in no time.'

'Right. But it's all something to think about, Harry. It wouldn't be easy operating the rotavator in the dark, not when you've got to walk behind it holding both handles to control it. That might rule out someone holding a torch and put the argument in favour of the van headlights. Maybe someone saw those lights? I'll ask around. Now, any ideas about the identity of the culprit?' I put to him.

He shrugged his shoulders. 'Search me. I haven't a clue.'

'Does anyone in Thackerston own a rotavator?' was my next question. Thackerston is a very small village and if someone living there did own or use a rotavator, Harry would know.

'Not to my knowledge. All our local farmers use ploughs, and this damage was never done with a plough. The cut's far too narrow and shallow for that. And most of our amateur gardeners hereabouts haven't got the money to splash out on something expensive like a rotavator when a spade'll do just as well.'

'Right. So my next question, Harry: motive. What is the motive? Has anybody been upset lately? A cricketer dropped from the team, perhaps? Someone thinking they should be the new captain, that sort of thing?'

He thought for a while, then shook his head.

'No, our lads aren't that way inclined. They're a team, Nick, a bunch of friendly chaps. They accept there's got to be changes and a few upsets, but they never take it to heart, not so as they'd do summat like this.'

'Now, it seems it was done during last night? Is that what you think?'

'Yes. Yesterday evening, I prepared the pitch for tonight, for our regular fortnightly home game. We're playing Elsinby. The field was fine when I left, Nick. I ran the cutter across the pitch and freshened up the white lines at the wickets. I finished about half-past eight; there was nobody about at that time.'

'So what about tonight's match? Will you be able to play?'

'Put it this way, we've played on far worse pitches in our time,

Nick, some still being used! If I think we can't play here, I'll have words with one of the nearby clubs. We might even use Elsinby's field if I can't fettle ours. But rest assured, we'll play somewhere, Nick, that's for sure. Luckily, the damage is across the centre of the pitch, it's not where the ball lands during bowling and I think we can cope with the uneven bits of the outfield. Once I get our roller on it and them turfs put back in place, you'll not see the joins. It'll take me all day, but I can spare the time just now; I've been able to postpone a plumbing job today.'

'So it's not as bad as it looks. Now, did anyone hear anything overnight? That rotavator would make quite a lot of noise while it was being used, and it must have been brought to the field somehow, by vehicle I guess, at some odd time of night. And there's the lights I mentioned. . . .'

'The field's tucked away behind the village hall, and that's on the edge of the village – folks never complain about music and dancing or the noise and traffic from functions, that's one reason the hall was built out there, so I doubt if anyone would have heard the rotavator or noticed the lights or seen anyone arriving in a vehicle at a strange time. I don't live far away and I never heard it.'

'I'll ask around the village,' I told him. 'I'll record this as a case of malicious damage, Harry. What is the cost of the damage, do you think?'

'Not a lot, Nick. I can fix it as I said. The fact that furrow goes across the pitch and not along it limits the damage. Even if we can't play here tonight, we'll be able to play on Saturday, definitely. We have a home fixture. But if you want a value, I'd say twenty pounds.'

'That'll do for my report,' I said.

I began my enquiries around the village of Thackerston paying special attention to the people who lived close to the village hall and cricket field, but elicited no useful information. Next, I paid a visit to every member of the cricket team, including the club officials and a handful of supporters, but nobody had heard or seen anything. I failed to discover a motive for the attack and likewise failed to find anyone in Thackerston who owned or had use of a rotavator. The unfortunate event was a total mystery. Thanks to the energetic and skilful work by Harry Wheater, Thackerston cricket pitch was fit for play that same evening; the match was a friendly, such games played early in the season being regarded as practice matches or opportunities to study the ability of new players.

And although watch was kept by club members overnight on Wednesday and Thursday, there was no further damage. I continued my enquiries in the district, and by the end of my shift on Friday, I had exhausted all my sources of enquiry. No one knew of a motive for the damage, no one had seen or heard the rotatavor at work, nor had they seen or heard the presence of a vehicle on the cricket field during the night hours. I drew a complete blank, but reported my efforts to Sergeant Blaketon.

He said, 'Well, Rhea, let's hope it's a one-off case of malicious damage. Even so, it might be an idea for our patrols – and you, of course – to visit all local sports fields during each night, just to make sure Rotavating Ronnie hasn't developed a passion for turning over cricket fields or anything else for that matter. And I hope it's not a determined cricket-hating fisherman looking for worms. I'll make sure our night patrols are aware of this, and in the coming week, you'd better have words with the cricket secretaries of all your local teams.'

'Very good, Sergeant.'

'Put them on the alert, Rhea, they might even initiate a night-watchman system.'

'I'm sure word will have got around anyway, Sergeant, but I'll warn them all officially.'

I managed to warn all the cricket club secretaries on my beat, most of whom said they either would or had already established a system of checks on their fields, even though it might not be possible to maintain these for very long.

But on the Saturday morning, the groundsman at Pattington cricket field went to inspect the pitch and found a gash right across the middle. Just like the one at Thackerston, it formed a giant letter J but this one did not cross the pitch at right angles. It did not run the length of the pitch either, but had been executed at an angle, slicing quite a large section of the beautifully prepared wicket area at the pavilion end. Although Pattington was not on my patch, it was on the adjoining beat and within my own sub-division, so I was called out to inspect it. My task was to compare the method of damage with that which had occurred at Thackerston.

'It's the same.' I was not in any doubt about that. 'A rotavator. And the damage is made in the shape of a letter J.'

Pattington cricket field was well away from the village, too, and when I asked the groundsman the same questions I'd asked Harry Wheater, I got the same answers. The Pattington constable, PC Derek Warner, was present during this and I acquainted him with the full facts of the Thackerston damage. He assured me he would make enquiries on his patch and inform me if he learned anything of value to my enquiries, particularly whether any of the team or their supporters had a grudge to air.

'How long would it take to do this?' was a question I had not considered, but it was one that Derek asked the Pattington groundsman, George Baxter.

'It's not dug very deep, as you can see,' George pointed out. 'Almost skimmed the surface but enough to cause deep cuts in the turf and turn some over. You can't play cricket on that. Time to do this? Not long. Ten minutes at the most, I'd say.'

'Right, I'll ask around,' said Derek Warner. 'And I'll see if any of our locals have a rotavator. I'll keep in touch, Nick.'

'Does this mean today's match is cancelled?' I put to George.

'Almost certainly,' he said. 'I don't think I can repair that wicket in time as we were due to start at two this afternoon. If the damage had been confined to the outfield, we might have managed. But the wicket's damaged, that'll take some time to repair and it needs doing properly. I'll have a look around for another venue, but that's never easy at short notice.'

Although only one of these acts of damage had been committed on my beat, both teams were within the same local cricket league, the Southern Moors. For that reason, I decided to circulate details to Eltering Sub-Divisional Headquarters so that all constables whose beats contained teams from that league were alerted. That initiative resulted in a telephone call from Inspector Breckon who quizzed me about the incidents and then said he would ensure that everything possible was done to locate the culprit and protect cricket pitches through the sub-division.

But we did not prevent the same thing happening at Crampton a week later. As there had been no midweek attempt upon any local cricket pitch, perhaps due to our high profile police patrolling, I think the league's clubs relaxed their vigilance and reduced their night watches. Crampton's splendidly maintained pitch, located within the grounds of Crampton Hall, had been attacked in precisely the same way as the others.

A rotavator had cut the surface of the grass in a diagonal furrow, once again affecting the wicket area and, like the others, it terminated in the hook of the letter J. On Saturday morning, the groundsman, Jeff Winters, rang me almost in tears.

'I'd just got it right, Mr Rhea, for the match with Lord Crampton's eleven this afternoon ... who'd do a thing like this?'

I drove down to Crampton and met him at the cricket field. Although it was within the grounds of Crampton Hall, there was a separate entrance and in fact the field was several hundred yards away from the big house, out of sight behind a hillock on top of which was a copse of sycamores. I found Jeff, who was employed as a gardener by Lord Crampton; he was now in the cricket pavilion, marching up and down in his frustration.

During our discussions, the familiar pattern emerged – an isolated cricket field, a club belonging to the Southern Moors League, the turf cut during the night with a rotavator in the form of a letter J, and no one had heard anything or seen anything untoward. Jeff could offer no suggestion as to a motive or a culprit, adding that Lord Crampton had been informed and had given Jeff time off this morning in the hope the pitch could be salvaged in time for this afternoon's game. In his case, the field was owned by Lord Crampton, but he let it to Crampton Cricket Club for a tiny rent, one of his contributions to the local community.

As I compiled the preliminary crime report in my office at home, I began to wonder whether the fields of every team in the Southern Moors League would eventually be attacked.

With this in mind, I cut a printed list of the league teams from the local paper and tucked it into my pocket book, marking those which had already been attacked; next, I examined their locations on the map, particularly as they related to one another in terms of distance and connecting roads, but I could not identify any particular association or relationship between the victims and any other team. I began to wonder if the culprit was nursing a grudge or a motive which was not linked specifically to the game. And yet it was someone who knew about local matches – every attack so far had occurred the night before a game. It seemed the idea had been to prevent that particular match. But why? At this early stage of the season, there was no championship or cup at stake and the pressure to achieve great things was not so great now as it would be towards the climax of the cricket season. To my knowledge, none of the threatened matches had been of any particular importance, a fact which made the rotavator raids even more peculiar.

It was at that point, I wondered who the opponents of the victimized clubs had been. The first, Thackerston, had been due to play a friendly match against Elsinby, but with the local weekly paper on my desk, it was easy to find out who Pattington's opponent had been last week. It was also Elsinby. I wondered if this was a coincidence, and then turned to the same paper for a list of this week's matches – and Lord Crampton's eleven was scheduled to play against Elsinby this Saturday afternoon. The three victimized clubs had all been due to play against Elsinby, also a member of the Southern Moors League. And they'd all been home matches – home to the victimized team, that is, and all due to be played the day following the raid.

I sensed that these factors suggested rather more than a mere coincidence and began to wonder if the clue to this problem lay within Elsinby cricket team – or a particular member of it. As my newspaper did not give me the fixtures for the following week, I would have to either obtain a fixture list from one of the clubs or have words with one of the local officials. I knew the captain of the Aidensfield team fairly well; he was Stan Calvert, a tall, fair-haired man who lived in the council houses. I guessed he would be playing somewhere this afternoon and, as he was not on the telephone, I hurriedly put on my cap and drove down to his house. He was having an early lunch when I arrived.

I explained the purpose of my visit and he listened carefully, then replied, 'Next weekend we're playing Elsinby.'

'At home or away?' I asked.

'At home,' he told me. 'On the Aidensfield ground.'

'Then you might be next on Rotavating Ronnie's list,' I warned him. 'He's always attacked the grounds the night before a match, and it's always been the ground of the team due to play against Elsinby. So I think we need to discuss some kind of overnight security for your cricket field, Stan.'

'Right, Nick, thanks for the warning. Look, I'm rushing off now. Come and see me later in the week; meanwhile, I'll get some mates to give us a hand.'

'Get them to keep it to themselves, Stan,' I warned him. 'I don't want Rotavating Ronnie to know we're onto him; I want to catch him in the act.'

'Fair enough.'

I told Sergeant Blaketon about my theories and he agreed with my proposals to lay a trap for Rotavating Ronnie; he would give me an extra hand in the shape of PC Alf Ventress and we would take up our positions from dusk on Friday evening. We would conceal ourselves on the cricket field to await developments.

But all that was in a week's time. During the interim period, I decided to make a few discreet enquiries in and around Elsinby, partly to ascertain if any member of the cricket team owned or had access to a rotavator, and partly to determine whether or not there was any internal political matter within the club which might have resulted in these attacks. So far as the rotavator was concerned, my very carefully conducted investigation showed that no member of the team owned such a machine, nor had any of them been known to borrow one. I had seen a full list of all club members, officials and players and could not point the finger of suspicion at any of them. The only snippet of gossip was that one of the team members, Miles Dyson, the fast bowler, had taken a shine to the away scorer, a stunning blonde 20-year-old girl called Moira O'Sullivan. Miles was unmarried and was a tall, rather dashing 25-year-old whose father ran some local racing stables. Miles did not work with horses nor indeed did he follow horse racing, preferring cricket as his sport, girls as his pastime, a bright red MG tourer as his means of transport and a career in advertising at York by which he earned enough money to finance his varied interests. Everyone thought he and Moira, a lithe blonde who lived with her parents at Longview House, Elsinby, and whose well-to-do father owned a chain of garages in the area, were ideal for one another.

They'd met when Miles had bought his latest car from one of the O'Sullivan group of garages, Moira being the receptionist at that particular outlet in Galtreford. My quiet enquiries did not show how this liaison might have led to the damage of cricket pitches. Having spent some time on these background investigations without producing any hint of a motive by anyone in the Elsinby club, I turned my attention once again to the rotavator. These two-stroke-fuelled, hand-controlled digging machines were not very common at that time and if there was one in the vicinity, then most of the gardening enthusiasts or allotment holders would know about it. But none did. I'd asked all over the area, even visiting local garages to see if anyone called regularly to buy fuel for a rotavator, but drew a blank.

Then, on the Friday of that week, I went to Ashfordly while I was off duty. I was due to work a late shift because tonight I'd be keeping observations on Aidensfield cricket field from around nine o'clock. I was due to begin my duties at 6 p.m., working through until 2 a.m. or until such time as we caught our rotavating rogue. I was in civilian clothes and had some banking to do as well as some shopping for decorating materials, my mission being to decorate one of our children's bedrooms. As the marketplace car-park was full, I sought some other convenient place and found myself in a short cul-de-sac fairly convenient for the town centre. As I drove in, I noticed some new premises: the sign said Ashfordly Agricultural, with a secondary one announcing repairs, maintenance and servicing to lawn mowers and other small agricultural machines. And in the window there was a new rotavator.

I could not miss the opportunity and went in. The owner, a breezy man in brown overalls, came to attend to me and when I expressed interest in the rotavator, he began to explain its merits and functions. His sales patter went on to say that these were becoming very popular with people who had large gardens and not a lot of time to tend them.

When I asked if anyone living nearby had bought one recently, he said, 'You're the bobby from Aidensfield, aren't you?'

'Yes, Rhea's the name.'

'Well, a chap near you at Ploatby's just got one, a couple of months back. He's delighted with it, you could always go and watch his in action if it's any help. He made that offer to me; he said he was breaking new ground – his little joke, I might add – but said if anyone wanted a practical demonstration, he'd be willing to give one.'

'That sounds a good idea. Who is he?'

'Walter Nelson, he lives at Sundial House, Ploatby. A fairly recent arrival in the village, I'm told, a chap in his fifties. I think he's something to do with the catering industry. He came here from Leeds. I think he owns a food distribution business. Very affable and friendly, a most obliging man. Nice wife and lovely red-haired daughter too. They've bought Sundial House. It was a bit run down and they're doing it up, making it like a palace and making a vegetable and herb garden out of the old lawn area. He's obviously got a bit of cash behind him.'

I thanked my new contact and decided that tonight, when I came on duty at 6 p.m. I would drive out to see what Mr Nelson could tell me about rotavators. He lived close to Elsinby – Ploatby was only a mile and a half away along a narrow country lane. I knew his name had not appeared on the list of Elsinby

Cricket Club members, players or officials and did not consider him a suspect. But then caution set in. I thought – if he is the only rotavator owner living near Elsinby and if he is a suspect, then my visit this evening – this very important evening – might alert him to my professional interest. He might not therefore launch his attack on Aidensfield cricket field which meant we would not catch him redhanded, and that would leave him free to continue his rotavating raids.

We had to stop him and the only way was to catch him in the act tonight. Somewhat reluctantly, I decided not to visit him this evening. If we did not catch the culprit, then I could call on him at some future date.

My first task after coming on duty at six was a brief chat with Stan Calvert, the Aidensfield captain; since I'd talked with him earlier in the week he'd recruited three volunteers to help keep watch on the cricket field, and I said they would be of great use in our bid to catch the Rotavating Ronnie. I arranged to meet Stan, his helpers and Alf Ventress behind the pavilion at eight o'clock. Each of us would be equipped with a powerful torch, a flask of coffee and something to eat. By the time we had made ourselves comfortable, darkness would have fallen and we'd be on site to plan a reception committee for our troublesome visitor. I had to explain that any arrests must be made by the police.

At the due time, we assembled as planned, Alf bringing his police vehicle on to the field to park it behind the pavilion well out of sight. He ensured it showed no lights, but it was needed to provide a means of communication during Operation Rotavating Ronnie. The plan was that the cricket field should appear to be absolutely normal which meant the access gate would be standing open. It always did stand open, but our plan was to have one volunteer concealed nearby; he would close and lock the gate the moment the rotavator was *in situ* and started. Stan had thoughtfully found a padlock and chain so that the gate could be locked. In that manner, we would contain both the rotavator and the vehicle in which it was transported. Even if the perpetrator managed to flee from the scene, we'd be able to seize his vehicle and the machine as evidence of his culpability. As our plan was put into operation, we decided that Alf would immobilize the vehicle by removing the ignition key and switching off the engine and lights; because I was the younger of the police officers present, I would carry out the arrest, if necessary by chasing the villain on foot, and our endeavours would be illuminated by our torches. The villain's arrest would follow as sure as night follows day.

I explained to our team that we had to allow the suspect to park on the field and then give him time to unload the rotavator, start it and even cut one or two slices of turf – only by that way could we prove his intention to cause damage. If we stopped him before he actually cut anything, he could deny all responsibility for the crime of malicious damage and I had to impress upon our volunteers that there was no criminal offence in merely driving a van and a rotavator onto a cricket pitch.

The civil offence of trespass was not a police matter. If we pounced too early and prevented him committing the crime, we'd have to let him go and, unless he made a voluntary confession, he'd never appear before a criminal court of law. Our plans made, therefore, we settled down for our indeterminate wait not knowing what time we would be called upon to display our arresting skills.

Nothing happened until after midnight. The parish church clock struck twelve and we began to wonder if our presence had been noticed, but then a pair of powerful headlights illuminated the skyline as a vehicle headed in our direction. It was the cue for total silence on the cricket field. Our gatekeeping volunteer, a portly gent called Ernie, scuttled around the boundary towards the open gate and concealed himself behind an elderberry bush as the lights approached. Soon, I could determine that it was a small vehicle and it was heading in our direction. I called out for stillness and silence; each of us knew our impending role and Alf's official radio was turned to its lowest volume. A hush descended upon Aidensfield cricket pitch.

Very shortly afterwards, the oncoming lights approached the gate and entered the field, the vehicle bouncing down the slight slope before coming to a halt with its lights blazing and its engine running.

'It's him!" breathed Alf Ventress. 'We've got him . . . caught in the act. . . .'

'Not yet, Alf,' I said. 'We haven't got him yet. Give him time. . . .'

'For God's sake don't let him ruin our pitch . . .' breathed Stan.

Whatever our suspect was doing, it seemed to be taking a long time, but eventually I saw a dark figure emerge from the van and go around to the rear doors.

I heard the doors being opened and this was followed by further noises which I understood to be some planks of wood being placed in position to form a ramp from the rear of the van to the ground, and then the unloading of the heavy rotavator. And all the time, the vehicle engine continued to run and the lights shone across the centre of the pitch. Once the rotavator was on the ground, we could hear the carburretor being primed and the starting handle being pulled; it spluttered into life with the chug-chug sounds of a two-stroke engine and we then saw the handler manoeuvre it towards the centre of the field. At this stage, it was not cutting the turf but was merely being wheeled into position.

'Now?' breathed Stan, thinking of his precious turf.

'Not yet,' I hissed. 'He's not digging yet . . . he must be caught digging, we've got to get evidence of damage. . . .'

It wasn't many minutes before the tone of the engine changed as the miniature ploughing system was put into operation; as it began to dig into the turf of the outfield, I hissed, 'Right, go, go go.'

Already, the gate had been closed; Alf Ventress ambled at his fastest speed in the darkness around the boundary as he made for the van while I made a bee-line for our suspect. One of the cricketing volunteers followed Alf as a back-up and another followed me for the same reason while Stan's job was to immobilize the rotavator, prevent further damage and make sure it was not removed by the suspect.

But, as we all ran towards our intended targets, the suspect heard our panting approach. He abandoned the rotavator and legged it into the all-embracing darkness.

I was now faced with the task of catching the swiftest-moving part of our quarry. Knowing the geography of the field very well indeed, I decided not to switch on my torch; in the reflections from the vehicle headlights, I could see well enough to pursue the dark, slender figure which fled before me and I was pleased to note that my helper emulated my actions. He did not put on his torch either and he knew the lay-out of the field very well indeed.

The figure was racing towards the village, no doubt thinking the gate was still open but then our temporary gatekeeper gave the game away by shouting something and waving his torch as the fleeing suspect approached. The result was that my quarry turned suddenly left and made for the railings which surrounded the field. Beyond was a patch of uncultivated land with trees and shrubs; if he got into that kind of natural cover, I could easily lose him. . . .

But I was gaining. I shouted for him to halt but this had no effect. I could hear the distressed, high-pitched panting of my quarry and then he tripped over a clump of grass as he left the smoothness of the cut field and entered the roughness of the surrounding area. That momentary stumble interrupted his flight and allowed me to gain precious ground. By the time he reached the wooden fence, I was close enough to risk a rugby tackle. I launched myself and managed to secure a firm grip around the thighs of my prey, just above the knees. This brought him tumbling to the ground with a high-pitched cry of alarm and terror and within seconds, I had secured an armlock. At this stage, my helper arrived, closely followed by Alf Ventress, Stan Calvert and the others.

But, as Alf's torch shone upon the face of our captive, we were amazed to find it was a young woman – and one I had never seen before. Of medium height and build with lovely auburn hair tied back in a pony-tail, she was dressed in dark denim overalls. I guessed she was in her early twenties. I was momentarily stunned by this, but recovered in time to chant the official caution before telling her she was being arrested for causing malicious damage to Aidensfield cricket pitch. She said nothing in reply.

'I'm taking you to Ashfordly Police Station,' I told her. 'What's your name? We need to contact your relatives.'

Again, she said nothing.

'We can trace them through the van's registration number,' I said. 'It's only a matter of time.'

By this stage of the proceedings, everyone had gathered around to look at the person responsible for these senseless acts of damage, and when I asked if anyone knew the girl, they all shook their heads.

'OK,' I said. 'Alf, you can drive me and the prisoner. . . .'

'Prisoner?' she spat like a cat. 'Prisoner? What do you mean, prisoner?'

'You are a prisoner,' I said firmly. 'You are under arrest for causing malicious damage and you will be subjected to the full weight of the law. You will now be taken to Ashfordly Police Station where you will be formally charged. Stan, leave the van and rotavator where they are for now. I'll take the van keys, and perhaps you can lock the gate when we've gone? That'll keep the van here until we remove it.'

'Sure, Nick. You will try to find out who she is and why she's done this?'

'We will,' I said, making sure I did not relax my grip on this woman.

To cut short a long story, she was Fiona Nelson, the daughter of Walter Nelson, the newcomer to Sundial House at Ploatby. It seems she had developed some kind of passion for Miles Dyson, the Elsinby fast bowler but he had shown absolutely no interest in her. The current focus of his attention was Moira O'Sullivan, the girl who acted as the scorer for Elsinby whenever they played away from home. When they played home games, the scorer was an elderly man called Jack Simpson who'd done the job for years, but who found it most difficult to cope with steps and difficult accesses at the away teams' premises. Moira had therefore volunteered to stand in for him during away matches.

Fiona, in her desperate attempt to get Miles to notice her, had hit upon the idea of sabotaging the pitches of the clubs who were hosting Elsinby's away matches, the idea being that Elsinby would have to play on another pitch, i.e. their own, and that Moira would not be there because she would not be scoring. She only came to cricket matches when she was scoring, so Fiona had discovered. This left the field open for Fiona, so she had calculated, but her first act of damage misfired because Thackerston played on the damaged pitch. Following that, Fiona made greater attempts to damage the wicket areas to enforce a change of venue. When I asked her about the significance of the letter J, she shook her head.

'It's nothing; I just went across the field and turned around to come home, then switched off the blades.'

In visiting her parents to compile her antecedent history, it seems they had moved to Ploatby because she'd got a fixation for a vicar at their previous address and insisted on going into the church to ring the bells as a sign of her undying love.

In our case, the lovesick Fiona was put on probation for two years by Eltering Magistrates and the bench made an order for her to repay the costs of any repairs. We all knew that her father would pay – he'd already made that offer. It was also a condition of her probation that she did not visit any of the cricket fields within the Southern Moors League over the next two years. I didn't think this restriction would trouble her too much because, in court, I did see her eyeing the rather dashing young journalist who was present in the Press gallery that morning.

'Well done, Rhea,' said Sergeant Blaketon when it was all over. 'It's funny what women will do in the pursuit of love.'

'She was a little on the simple side,' I said. 'She's a nice girl, but the family have problems with her. She keeps falling in love and letting the whole world know about it when things go wrong.'

'So Rotavating Ronnie was a woman after all. Well, it's finished, Rhea. In some ways, you've got to feel sorry for a girl like that. And her parents, of course. And did you know that rotavator is a palindrome, Rhea? A word spelt the same backwards as it is forwards? Probably the longest such word in our language?'

'And did you know that the longest known palindrome in the English language is 'Dog as a devil deified; deified lived as a god,' I asked.

He smiled. 'Or, as Napoleon is reputed to have said, "Able was I ere I saw Elba!"'

To which I added, 'And as Adam said when he met Eve – Madam, I'm Adam.'